Tango in Italian

YLVA KAISER

Tango in Italian

Publisher: BoD – Books on Demand, Stockholm, Sweden
Printer: BoD – Books on Demand, Norderstedt, Germany
ISBN: 978-91-8057-236-1

Forse non sarà una canzone
A cambiar le regole del gioco
Ma voglio viverla così quest'avventura
Senza frontiere e con il cuore in gola

E il mondo in una giostra di colori
E il vento che accarezza le bandiere
Arriva un brivido e ti trascina via
E sciogli in un abbraccio la follia

Notti magiche inseguendo un goal
Sotto il cielo di un'estate italiana
E negli occhi tuoi voglia di vincere
Un'estate, un'avventura in più

Quel sogno che comincia da bambino
E che ti porta sempre più lontano
Non è una favola e dagli spogliatoi
Escono i ragazzi e siamo noi

Notti magiche inseguendo un goal
Sotto il cielo di un'estate italiana
E negli occhi tuoi voglia di vincere
Un'estate, un'avventura in più

Edoardo Bennato & Gianna Nannini, ***Un' Estate Italiana***
Official anthem of the FIFA World Cup, Italy 1990

(English translation)

Maybe it won't be a song
To change the rules of the game
But I want to live this adventure like this
Without borders and with your heart in your throat

And the world in a carousel of colours
And the wind caressing the flags
A thrill comes and drags you away
And dissolves madness in an embrace

Magical nights chasing a goal
Under the sky of an Italian summer
And in your eyes the desire to win
One summer, one more adventure

That dream that begins as a child
And that takes you further and further
It's not a fairy-tale and from the locker room
The boys come out and it's us

Magical nights chasing a goal
Under the sky of an Italian summer
And in your eyes the desire to win
One summer, one more adventure

Chapter 1

I drive the grey, nondescript rental car down the coastal road from the airport, fussing over how the automatic transmission does not shift gears as quickly as I would prefer, the engine whining in protest as it struggles to catch up with my demands. My clothes already stick to the seat in the flimsy air condition, and I roll all four windows down, the pleasantly warm September air sweeping through the compact little Fiat and tossing my hair around in a way that almost – almost – makes me imagine away the roof of the car and the annoying way it blocks the raw sunshine. It is a shame company policy does not allow me to rent a convertible, since this weather and this road are both essentially screaming for it. I press down on the accelerator, the tires screeching with friction as I pull them around the serpentine bends leading down to the rocky white outcrop upon which Ancona perches. From above, its natural harbour appears shaped like a claw, protectively folded around the cove as if daring anyone to attempt to breach it. The pale terracotta silhouette of the cathedral, standing proud at the highest point of town, holds my gaze as I swivel past.

The production facilities are located on the north side of town, while the hotel rests to the south, where the coastline is wilder, yet more tranquil, green forestry scrambling up white, craggy cliffs. I have never been here in high season, but I imagine it will get far more crowded than this. The complex seems huge; apart from the oblong buildings lining the waterfront, where my room is located, there is an elevated section, almost like a tower, but I cannot tell whether it is even in use at this time of year. There are no lights in the windows, and I have yet to see anyone enter or leave.

I lean over the balcony, the breath of the sea on my skin. The white rocks turn pink in the receding sunlight, the impression that of quartz crystals scattered at random across the shore.

Inside, the TV is on, panoramic views of the hotel rolling by in a slideshow to supposedly soothing music. I switch the channel, past a news reel in rapid Italian, a similarly unintelligible talk show and some form of documentary on sailing, pausing briefly on the sports channel, recapitulating highlights from the final round of qualifiers for next summer's European football championship. I start unpacking while I watch the summary of goals and missed chances – one of France's is particularly hideous – and make a mental note that I ought to call Mike about buying tickets. This time the championship will be held in England, and missing out would be equivalent to asking to have your citizenship revoked. Though it has been years since he played himself, he does sometimes kick about with friends' children or younger cousins, to their immense glee, and both of us are as childishly involved every time there is a big tournament.

I toss my travel T-shirt away and collect my hair in a bun, relishing the thought of a warm shower. Travelling with hand luggage means there is not much to unpack, but I do find hangers for my blazer and work blouse. It might be silly, but feeling well-dressed inspires confidence, and wearing a blazer always seems to improve the quality of my presentations. It is almost as if even I take myself more seriously.

My phone vibrates with a text from Rachel, and I glance up.

Hey, it says. **Hope you arrived safely. I don't want to ruin your day, but... well. There is something you need to see, and it is probably better to give you fair warning.**

There is a link to a Facebook post, and even as I click on it, a nasty feeling is settling in my stomach. *Do I really want to see this?* Probably not. In fact, maybe I should just...

Too late. The page opens to a half-blurry picture from what looks like a party, the background dim and filled with beer glasses on a high table. I cannot tell if it is a pub or at someone's house. What I can tell is that there are people in the foreground, seemingly drunk dancing, except for two of them, who are busy making out. One of whom happens to be Nathan, my so-called boyfriend.

I scroll down the post and realise it is from his own account. As in, not just a drunken mishap. At least not one he regrets. *Great. Just great.*

I know we have not been seeing each other for that long, and that I was not all that certain of where this was going, yet it hurts more than I thought it would. Somehow, I am not surprised, because this is how it usually ends. And still, I just hoped it would perhaps be different, this time. He did tell me, only last week, how much he liked me. *Was that a complete lie, or do some people actually change their minds that fast?*

I'm sorry, Rachel writes. **I just thought you should know**.

Yeah, thanks, I write back. Then, after a moment's hesitation, **Wish you were here, even though you probably wouldn't have had that much to do.**

You know I'm excellent at wasting away time in the sunshine, the reply comes. **Wish I was there too honey. That appalling Abbott-Smythe family is coming in today.**

Ah, joy. Who would have thought interior design could be so detrimental to mental health? Don't let them push you around. Especially that horrid woman with the pink leopard coat. That alone should be illegal.

I won't. Will let you know later if I'm still alive or if I overdosed on lunch G&T's. Take care and enjoy!

Enjoy, I think to myself. *As if.* Although that idea had indeed occurred to me, that this would be some form of working vacation, or at least that I would have time to relish the extended summer, Nathan's post leaves a foul taste in my mouth. It really would have felt better to have Rachel with me, as a partner in crime, a pillar to lean on. Anything, really, to prevent myself from being holed up in my own mind. I should probably work, to keep myself distracted, but I know myself well enough to recognise that it will only make me more annoyed.

As the sun sets, I head up to the terrace for a glass of wine, catching the last rays of light as they disappear over the horizon, hues of bonfire orange gradually shifting to blood red before they fully plunge into darkness. I swirl my glass, letting the final sparks reflect in the white wine, turning its already warmly yellow tone golden. The waiter tells me the grape is Trebbiano, commonly grown in this region. It is crisp and mineral, with subtle hints of lemon. Most of all, it disappears all too quickly, same as the fading light. My mind drifts, unbidden, to Nathan's post and I order another. It is unsettling, the way I cannot seem to push it from my mind. I think back on the first time we met, our easy conversation, his contagious laughter, how he insisted on paying for lunch, which turned out to last six hours and end in a grappa tasting. While my tongue curls at the memory of the tart, petrol sensation of the liquor, the gesture lingers. Guys showering me with acts of affection have been rare to say the least, and I reluctantly acknowledge a part of me might be somewhat starved.

What changed? I ask myself. *Was it something I did? Or something I didn't?*

Immediately, I despise myself. *Why do I blame myself, when he is the one who has been cheating?* Yet the feeling is difficult to shake. I think of my boss, urging me to analyse every situation one step further. "Why do you think this person reacted in this manner?" he might say. "It was unnecessary, yes, but what provoked it? What could you have done to prevent it?"

"Read minds", I mutter to myself as I sip my wine. "Anticipate bullshit." The sun is long gone now, the night as black as my soul. Distractedly, I wonder whether it is possible to understand another person entirely. If you can ever expect them to live up to what they make themselves out to be.

I suppose it would make sense to cry, but somehow my eyes remain dry. I am not sad as much as disappointed. Dispirited, disillusioned. *Here we go again.* I do not expect much, these days, but even so, it is apparently possible to be negatively surprised.

Almost in compulsion, I flip through my phone, noticing nothing of interest as much as the resounding absence of human contact. I gaze into the oblivion, willing it to speak to me, but even the void is silent.

Sleep is unruly, once I force myself into bed. There are people with knives, floodgates rising, flashlights swiping through the dusk in search of a murderer. Then the more familiar, but no less disturbing: the impression of a teenage girl's bedroom, floral and innocent, imploding in on itself, collapsing into a bottomless nothing.

I open my eyes to darkness, waiting for my heartbeat to return to normal. My back hurts from the unfamiliar bed and the far too stiff pillows and from curling up on itself in cramps. My phone flashes at 03:50.

It has been going on for a while, these dreams and these nights of disrupted rest. Some would certainly attribute it to stress, of one kind or another, but I do not feel stressed. I only feel empty, deflated, sick of everyone and everything.

Freud would have a ball with this, I find myself thinking.

I groan, throwing my arm over my eyes, before weariness overwhelms me.

Chapter 2

People tend to talk up hotel breakfasts to no end, but the fact of the matter is that however lavish, these buffets are remarkably overrated when you are on your own. I order a double espresso, then walk aimlessly along the tables, filled to the brim with exquisite cheeses, Parma ham, fresh fruit, all imaginable forms of bread, sweet and not sweet, eggs made to your preference, and a veritable mountain of ricotta, sitting in the middle of it all like a snow-capped peak. In the end, I order an omelette and nibble it distractedly while I scroll my phone for the news and work emails. Eventually, when the omelette has run its course and my coffee cup is sadly empty, I move out to the terrace, where at least I can savour the heat of the sun although the stark light makes me squint to see my computer screen, and feel slightly less depressed. I finished preparing the presentation for today's meeting weeks ago, and I have seen the slides so many times I think I would be able to draw them from memory, if I only had any artistic skills whatsoever. Nevertheless, I go over them yet again, make mental notes, answer a few emails despite the "out of office" automatic reply banner that is clearly displayed across my screen.

By the time the sun has moved behind the far side of the complex, I figure it is about time I start moving. It is only a short drive, but traffic here is unpredictable at best. Gathering up my things into my bag, I glance at my watch, then, longingly, over at the coffee machine. I could use another one of those if I am to get through this day. I still have time, and there are hardly any other guests here, just the one guy hanging around by the bar, seemingly without ordering anything. I hoist the bag up on my shoulder and walk over, reaching for my wallet.

That is when I realise that the man standing by the bar looks familiar. So familiar, in fact, that I allow myself a second glance. And…

Holy shit.

I know this guy. Or rather, I know who he is. All too well. *Shit shit shit.*

What the hell is Nicolo Di Luca, Italian international and AC Milan professional football player, doing right here, in my hotel?

Right, the Euro qualifiers. *Weren't they only a few days ago?* They must have played somewhere nearby. I had been watching England qualify over at Nathan's and – *damn it, don't think about him. Don't go there.* I shake my head to clear my thoughts. Anyway, what would I be doing thinking of Nathan when last year's 'Best Midfielder of the Serie A' is right here in this room?

My mind is spinning. I cannot even count off the top of my head the number of times I have seen this guy do ridiculous things on the pitch. Immediately, my thoughts go out to Mike. My brother would have committed murder to be in my shoes right now, given all the times he has been screaming his head off at some outrageous pass or cross into the box from the man in question. He is not the type to score many goals, but when he does, it is always spectacular. Most of all, it is the way he reads the game, the way he seemingly always knows where his teammates and opponents are in order to execute the best possible move…

Without noticing, I seem to have drifted closer. My hand is resting on the side of the bar as I try – and probably fail – to casually lean against it. I glance over, even as I try not to be too obvious. I signal to the barista to get me an espresso, even though caffeine is now probably the last thing that I need given the rate at which my pulse is racing. I swallow, eyeing him out of the corner of my eye. He is not much taller than I, but his lean build and something about his general aura – or my distorted imagination – makes it feel like he is towering over me. His dark brown hair coils down his neck, not exactly long but longer than I would normally approve of in a man. Yet somehow, it suits him. It falls into his eyes as his head tips down to look at his phone, and I find myself swallowing at the way it frames his face. The watch on his wrist looks sleek and tasteful enough to probably be outrageously expensive, its dark grey face contrasting neatly against his tanned skin.

"Your coffee, *signora*", the barista says, drawing my attention. I nod, unable to focus entirely on him, my eyes darting uncontrollably to my side even though I try to be subtle. He does not say anything, thankfully, but I can tell from the smirk passing over his features that he knows exactly what I am looking at.

"*Grazie*", I manage. Sipping my coffee, I eye him over the rim of the cup. It appears as if he is waiting for someone, the way he just idly hangs around, glancing interchangeably at his watch – *most likely the price of my car* – and his phone. At least he seems to have nothing better to do at this particular moment. I steel myself, swallowing the innate shame that rises in my throat. *What the hell, he is just a normal guy, like everyone else.* Except, not really, because clearly the average person is not capable of scoring directly from a corner kick. *Never mind that now.* I put my empty cup down on the counter, a little too forcefully, and in the process manage to make him look up. Straight at me, who in all honesty could have done with another minute or five to steady myself.

"I… Hi." I smile, nervously, while my stomach is doing triple backflips inside. "I don't mean to bother you. This feels really awkward and all, but…" I swallow, sheepishly, before blurting, "I really love to watch you play."

"Thank you", he says, and while he must be hearing this kind of thing from random – and not so random – people every day, there is a kind look in his eyes. At least he does not look like he is about to sigh dramatically and brush me off straight away. He has a nice voice, too, I notice. Deep and smooth, somehow reassuring.

“I… I… Hold on. Just a minute.” I roam around in my bag, frantically, searching for anything that might serve. I dare not look up until my hands close around my calendar, and even then, I feel embarrassed as I hand it over.

“I’m sorry”, I say, flinching, “that’s the best I have. I am here for work.” I shrug, apologetically, but he does not seem to mind. He takes it, almost delicately opening the first page, flipping past all the contact details and password notes I should probably not be showing around in public, and I watch, entranced, as he signs his name with a flourish. *I’ll never be able to get rid of that calendar now.*

“What do you do?” he asks, startling me. I look up, and find his eyes trained on me. Dark brown, with a faint speck of green, if the light is not playing tricks on me. It indeed might be, because I do feel slightly faint.

“I…” I stutter, caught off guard. *Dear lord, get a grip.* “I work with vaccine development. I am here to oversee one of our production sites, and do quality control on their procedures.” I shrug. *Don’t overdo it, you don’t even know if he knows what QC is.*

“That sounds interesting”, he says. “And important.” He raises an eyebrow. “A lot of people don’t know how many lives are saved by vaccines every year. It’s a good thing you’re doing.”

I try to hide the surprise that must be visible on my face. I guess I had half expected most athletes – exceptionally fit, innately healthy, commonly uneducated – to not give two cents about vaccinations, probably believing themselves half immortal and immune to everything. Moreover, I realise, as silly as it is, that it makes me glad to hear a person I admire say that he finds my work important. *Again, get a grip.* But there is something inquisitive in his gaze that does not let me relax.

“I had the shingles vaccine only recently”, he goes on, continuing to surprise me. “My brother-in-law was sick with it the other year, and he said it was horrible. I didn’t want to take the risk.” He cocks an eyebrow. “That’s not one of those you are working on, is it?”

"No", I say, swallowing, "but I know a couple of people, back from when I was at university, who do." *Are we seriously talking about this?*

"So, you're a doctor?" He has long since stopped writing in my calendar, but he is still holding it, and while he must be heading somewhere, and I probably should too as I have a schedule to adhere to and no idea what the time is, I cannot make myself ask for it back.

"My degree is in molecular biology", I say, wincing at how incredibly pretentious it sounds. "Spent quite a few years in a lab, growing cells and doing experiments…" *Sounds cute, the way you say it. As if it wasn't the seventh circle of hell, eighteen-hour workdays for a salary that would make a gas station attendant laugh his ass off.* "…to understand what causes disease so that we can help patients, or, ideally, to prevent disease altogether." I smile. *I am such a nerd. What does he care? He kicks a ball for a living. Just shut up.* "So, yes, I am a doctor, but not that kind of doctor."

"Impressive", he says. "My mother always wanted me to be a doctor. You know, something *useful*." He shrugs. "But I guess you have to be better with numbers than I was."

"Well, you had ten league goals and fourteen assists last year, nothing wrong with those numbers. Although I do think the one against Hellas Verona wasn't offside after all, so it should have counted as well."

Fuck. It is out of me before I can even react. *Why the hell did I say that?*

"Maths was never my strongest side either", I try to cover up.

He looks at me for a moment, and it is all I can do not to crumble to the floor.

"You *are* good with numbers", he finally says, smiling, and that smile sends a nerve firing inside me, straight from my brain into the pit of my stomach and all the way down between my legs. I realise I have been anatomically unaware of its existence right up until this point, but as fascinating as that is, I am unable to focus on anything else than how my body screams in silence. I do not know what to do with myself, and I have never been so acutely aware of my failure at rational thought ever before. It is fantastic, and exhilarating, and deeply and profoundly unnerving.

Say something, my brain urges me, with a note of desperation. *Anything.*

But I cannot. There is no way, no words big enough, or comprehensive enough, or even remotely appropriate, for what I feel in this moment.

Go on, say something, my brain pleads. As in, *I cannot take this anymore.*

"Practice makes perfect", I say, my voice a barely audible rasp that underperforms massively, but it is the best I have, because I can barely comprehend how I am still standing. I have no idea what just happened, only that I have never before felt this unbalanced, and I cannot for the life of me tell whether it is a good or a bad thing.

"I am sure", he says. He hands the calendar back, and I understand the conversation is over, the moment has passed, and I can only be left wondering for how long my brain decided to exit reality. A few minutes? Twenty? Half a day? My insides feel like mush.

"Thank you", I say, fighting with myself. "It was nice to meet you."

"You too, Sienna", he says, and it is not until he is gone, the room suddenly feeling vast in size as the space his presence occupied – so much larger than it ought to be for any single person – is rendered vacant, that I never actually told him my name.

Chapter 3

I do not know how I get through the meetings, but I do, although I fear some of my brain cells may never have entered the building. I move on autopilot, still reeling from what happened back at the hotel, and almost miss my floor despite having been here so many times I could probably draw the emergency exit plan from memory. The complex is sleek and modern, large floor-to-ceiling windows overlooking a vast open field flanked indefinitely by the ocean. It is built close to the hospital, visible around the corner with its nondescript off-white square structures reflecting the sunlight. The meeting room is equipped with state-of-the-art video conferencing equipment and equally advanced coffee-making facilities, but the interior designer clearly breezed over the ergonomics course as the chairs are flat-out murderous. I move around restlessly, desperately striving to find a position where my butt does neither cramp nor fall asleep, and where my spine does not become etched on my skin in the form of bruises.

"Dr Archer, would you mind going through the procedure once more on the board?"

I practically jump at the offer, wincing slightly as the ghastly chair releases me from its talons, and straighten myself as best I can as I run through the new procedures, the protocol amendments developed globally that will be a pain to adhere to, and the results of the QC done so far. The laboratory data is sound, but this is all about repetition, repetition, repetition. When you are working with the health and safety of other human beings, there is no room for error.

"Any questions?" I finish, doing my best to maintain a calm and inviting smile even though my head is filled to the brim with information and starting to ache. I really should start taking notes during these meetings, but it seems a skill lost to me, the extent of my failure to scribble down anything coherent exponentially proportional to the number of years that have elapsed since I received my degree. *Having a PhD doesn't actually increase your brain size,* I scold myself, *nor your memory storage space.* I sip on my third espresso of the day and try to sort through the disorganised jumble in my mind.

At the break, I find myself chatting to one of the Italian site managers, Luigi. I know his wife is in life science too, working for another company in another field. He gestures in his typical flippant manner as he sips his coffee standing up.

"This new batch of the influenza vaccine", he prompts, "it is promising. Very high yields and specificity." I nod.

"We need to ensure you – we – can keep it up though. It would be a huge advantage, obviously, being able to provide pan-influenza protection rather than the single-strain variant we offer every year, but we must be humble in that we have yet to figure out how long immunity lasts. It's likely that we will still have to provide repeated immunisations, but with a broader coverage, it might still be preferrable." This is something I am proud of. I know this is a strong product, with a definite public health advantage, but most of these people are first and foremost salesmen; they will never quite understand the true medical value of this innovation, however much I explain it. My job is to simplify it as much as possible while managing to convey the revolutionary essence of the product.

"Of course, of course", Luigi quips, nodding. I can tell Euro signs are rotating on his retina as we speak. "Everyone is very excited to get started. This is a huge thing for our site."

"I'm glad", I say, meaning it. My team have worked on this for so long and having come this far is a huge success. Still, it ought to feel more exciting than it does. My response comes out flat and it bothers me.

"So how is your boyfriend?" I look up. Frowning, I realise I must have told him about Nathan's existence in a weak moment, one which I now inwardly curse.

"Oh, no… Um, I, we… We're not…" I wave my hand around vaguely, not making any sense. "There is not much to say, really."

"And you travel so much, too", he says sympathetically. "It must be difficult when you see each other so rarely."

I grimace. I have never thought of it that way.

"It is my job", I say, disbelievingly. "How am I otherwise supposed to do this?"

"Perhaps he felt left behind." Luigi shrugs, leaning against the table. "Men tend not to like that."

"You mean they don't like women who have their own careers?" I shoot back, knowing full well I should not get into this conversation and that it does me no favours whatsoever. Cultural differences I can handle, but there are limits to my sense of diplomacy and I need to keep them in check. Luckily, Luigi only chuckles.

"Not like that, no. But I have never known a man who does not want his woman to long to come back to him. A woman who travels alone for work…" He shrugs. "The signal is pretty clear; she does not need him."

"Well, it's not so much about what I need as about what I must. He should be glad that if I do come back, it's because I want to, not because I need to."

"Ah, but you see", Luigi says, "that is exactly the problem. This leaves you with the decision, which is precisely what he cannot handle."

By the time I return to the hotel, exhaustion threatens to pull me under. I glance towards the restaurant, white linen billowing in the evening breeze, and find I cannot bear to spend another instant there alone. Instead, I stop by the bar, leaning against the counter to keep my head from spinning. I cannot remember the last time I ate.

The bartender – thankfully not the same as this morning – hands me a glass of water on a napkin and asks for my order. I point to a slice of *pizza al taglio* and devour it standing, the thick bread and molten cheese a comforting cushion in my belly.

In the elevator, I lean back, resting my head against the wall. My eyes close, as if by their own accord, and I exhale a long, unsteady breath. Slowly, I feel my pulse settling, the sensation of vertigo gradually dissipating. Struggling to compose myself, I fumble in my pocket for my phone, daring myself to skim through my emails.

The elevator doors have almost closed, but then a hand sticks through the crack and forces them back up. I glance up from my phone, briefly.

It is him.

My eyes meet his as the doors close behind him, shutting us in, into a world of our own.

"What floor?" I croak, eventually, when it has been quiet for what feels like an eternity. I have nothing better to say.

"Three", he says, his eyes still on me, and I swallow as I manage, "Same as me."

We travel the floors in silence, a tense silence – or maybe it is just my imagination, for why would he find it tense? Why would he care at all? We are just strangers sharing an elevator. The only awkwardness is the fact that I know who he is and the name of his sister and where he grew up and his season statistics, not to mention that I asked him to sign my work calendar, for lack of anything more appropriate, some hours ago.

After several years, the elevator comes to a halt, the doors sliding open. He motions for me to go first, so I do, reluctantly, because despite my inner panic, I neither can nor want to look away from him. I walk along the corridor, vaguely aware of his presence behind me. By my door, I stop, waving my key card about ridiculously.

"This is me." I do not know what else to say, however much I want to.

He points down the hall. "My room is just down there. Fancy a drink? It's not that late." Sensing my hesitation, which is, in reality, only pure shock, he adds, "Unless of course you have other plans..."

I cannot tell if he is being serious or not. I cannot tell if I am dreaming or not. But I can tell my feet are moving by their own accord, following him to the door at the end, so close behind him while he unlocks it that the overwhelming sensation of him comes over me again. A faint, yet powerful scent lingers in the air where he has just been, trailing after him. An intriguing hint of citrus, fresh and clean, yet with an undertone that is difficult to pinpoint, elusive and enigmatic, except that it is heavier, huskier, and very distinctly male.

The room is about three times the size of mine, at the corner of the building, with a double-sided terrace reaching out to the ocean. Off to my right there is a large bathroom, and what looks suspiciously like a built-in sauna.

He opens the fridge – not a minibar, an actual full-size fridge – and pulls out a bottle of champagne, already unscrewing the cap around the cork in one, fluid motion. I watch his hands as they wrap around the cork, preventing air and precious bubbles from escaping. He has beautiful hands, I cannot help but notice, the fingers long and slender, their gestures precise yet delicate.

The whole scene is so laid back yet absurdly romantic I cannot comprehend it is happening but also cannot help being swept away.

He gestures to the terrace through the open doors, and I grasp my glass the way a drowning man clutches at a buoy as I walk out into the temperate evening. A footpath leads down to the sea, where craggy rocks pierce the surface like the vicious teeth of an animal. A folded parasol flutters slightly in the breeze, but there are hardly any sounds – this is far from the main beach to where most guests head. These cliffs are secluded, as if shy.

I sip my champagne; the bubbles are exquisite, petite, elegant. I revel in the taste, reminiscing baked brioche, apples, and caged sunshine. I take another sip, to calm my nerves, before facing my host.

He stands behind me, just a few steps away, staring down into his drink as if lost in thought. Once he senses my gaze on him, he looks up, his features relaxing.

"Cheers", he says, raising his glass to toast mine, and I cannot help but smile.

"How did your work meetings go?" he asks, and I marvel at the fact that he has even considered what I did after he left this morning. Even so, I tell him, in so many words, what transpired, what the purpose was, deliberately leaving out my overall sense of confusion, attributable solely to the man in front of me. He nods, sips his champagne, asks questions far more insightful than I could have imagined.

"My brother-in-law is a dentist", he says by way of conversation. "He goes to plenty of conventions, and I get to hear him talk about medical things at dinner sometimes." He smiles wryly. "Though I figure what you do is far more advanced." And I do not know what to say to that, even though I silently agree.

"So what are you doing here?" I enquire in return. "Congrats on qualifying for the Euros, by the way. But shouldn't you be back in Milan by now?" Given that I have already revealed how closely I have watched his games, I figure there is no use denying that I know where he plays. He shrugs.

"We got two extra days off, and our next game isn't until Monday anyway. I went to see some friends."

It seems such a casual thing to do, yet I do not question it. There is something else nagging on my mind, a question far greater, that makes far less sense.

I lean against the railing, my elbows resting against the wood, my back against the soft lull of the sea.

"Why did you invite me in?"

He shrugs, and it is as if a sudden streak of insecurity sweeps over his features. Then it is gone again, in an instant, so fast I wonder if it was ever there.

"It was the way you looked at me", he says, sipping his champagne, levelling his gaze at me.

I expected a half-laugh, a cocky *so you mean didn't really want to be here?* or a matter-of-fact *because I could* or even a challenging *why not?* Not this. Tentatively, I raise an eyebrow.

"I am fairly sure people look at you all the time, wherever you go", I say, slowly, but I do not let my gaze waver from his.

"Not like that, they don't." He edges closer, his hips at a height with mine, his eyes still trained on me. I swallow.

"How is that, then?" Despite the champagne my mouth is suddenly so dry it comes out as a whisper.

"Like…" He seems to struggle for words, his accent suddenly more pronounced. "With meaning. Feeling."

Wonder, I almost fill him in. *Admiration. Longing.* But I cannot form a single comprehensive word as he takes another step towards me, setting his champagne glass down on the railing, swaying slightly in the breeze. He leans against it, arms on either side of me, and the world comes to a standstill – the wind hesitates, birds hover mid-air, the waves rise but refrain from breaking.

Then his hands find their way around my neck, slipping slowly, sensually into my hair, irrevocably sending shivers down my spine. His touch is soft, and gentle, yet every fraction of his skin on mine feels like lightning, like fire. I am so physically aware of his closeness every part of my body seems on edge. My hands travel up his neck in response, into his hair, my fingers marvelling at the silky softness between them even as my tongue explores his, and I feel my blood throbbing at the base of my throat, in the pit of my stomach, and everywhere in between. One hand resting on my hip, his thumb eases beneath my shirt, its touch featherlight on my heated skin.

His lips move to my neck and I lean back, giving him space. His fingers trail along my spine, and I find myself pulling him closer, urgently, almost desperately. A single thought goes through my head, determined, decisive. *Screw Nathan. If he can, then so can I.* What is more, he never made anything feel like this.

Truth be told, I realise as he takes a step back, inhaling sharply, I have *never* felt anything remotely like this, with anyone.

We face each other, and it is as if something passes between us, unspoken. He smiles, and it is a smile full of confidence, of shrewd mischief, yet pure and playful as he holds out his hand, the question clear in his eyes. I take it, and follow him inside. The bedroom doors open to both sides, white curtains billowing like swan wings. He wraps his arms around me from behind, kissing my neck, my shoulder. Excruciatingly slowly, his hands travel up my waist to the zipper in my blouse, and the despite the heat I shiver as it comes undone. He hovers there, for a moment, as if asking permission, as if I could make this stop even if I wanted to. Instead, I reach for his hand, guiding it to the straps, and they fall to the floor, along with everything else, while he drops tender kisses against my bare skin.

Suddenly self-conscious, I hardly dare look at him as I reach for the buttons in his shirt. I have nothing strictly to be ashamed of, even if I wish my waist was more pronounced and that I had chosen different underwear. Still, I do not want to know how many other women have been in this situation, and how much better they would have looked on a swimsuit edition magazine cover. But he places a finger beneath my chin, forcing me to look up.

I take him in where he stands, in nothing but black briefs, and let escape an involuntary sigh. His narrow waist, his tanned skin, the sleek outline of his muscles.

"What?" he whispers, and there it is again, that flicker of uncertainty, that shadow of doubt I thought I glimpsed earlier.

Unable to speak, I shake my head, reaching out, gingerly, to touch him.

"You're perfect", I breathe, my fingertips resting lightly against his chest.

And then he is on me, both of us laughing at the sudden lunge that sends us both toppling, ungraciously, onto the bed. He leans over me as he kisses me, palms spread on the stark white sheets, sinew and muscle visible beneath the skin in a way that makes me wish I had studied more anatomy.

Then his hand slips between my legs, those slender, steady fingers, sensitive yet determined, and I cannot stifle a gasp.

"Does it feel alright?" he murmurs against my throat, and I only manage to nod, my fingers tangling in his hair, my breath shallow. His mouth traces my neck, my hands the muscles in his back, and as he keeps caressing me, I break a fundamental, unspoken rule of my own – I call his name. It feels as ridiculous as I always thought it would, but I cannot stop myself – it is as if I am no longer in sole control of my own body. I feel him smiling against my throat, his tongue lightly tracing my collarbone; that beautiful, mischievous smile that only enhances the sensation mounting within. I close my eyes and grab for something – anything – to hold on to, and then his other hand is there, weaving into mine, and I clutch it with all my strength as I let go. It is a thunderstorm, an earthquake, an avalanche. It is electricity through my nerves, it is fire through my core. I tremble in his arms and bury my face in his shoulder and moan against his skin, and most of all I yearn for him to do it again, again, again.

At some point we run down to the ocean, racing to be the first to dive in, heedless of the rocks beneath the foaming water, the champagne bottle, now empty, resting on the cliffs as if in a drunken haze of its own. I wrap my arms around him, then my legs, as the dark waves crash over us and his kiss warms me from within. Afterwards, in the shower, the water is hot, the tiles along the wall cold, and our hands everywhere.

He is everything I have ever wanted and everything I will never have. The realisation should not come as a surprise but yet the notion that he could do this every week, have this same experience with another girl in another town, hurts more than it has any right to. The attraction is so strong it boils over into actual emotion, into serious care. My heart aches at the thought of never experiencing this ever again, yet my body is being rational, urging me to make the most of it while I still can. In this stolen moment in time, this wormhole in space created by sheer adoration and lucky chance.

When we finally fall asleep, it is with our bodies entwined, the sheet tangled between us, my arm around his neck, his around my waist. For the first time in as long as I can remember, I do not dream at all.

Chapter 4

To the soft lull of water, my mind gradually surfaces, an obscure whitewashed mass slowly emerging into focus. The sound is soothing, occasionally broken through by something I struggle to define, though the image that comes to mind is that of a sailboat, sails bulging, straining against the untameable force of the wind. Around me, foreign smells tease my imagination, salt and citrus mixing with faint undertones of sweat and washing powder from starched sheets.

I lie on my back, watching the ceiling materialise, realising as it does that this is not the ceiling of my flat back in Victoria Wharf. Neither are the half-open glass doors, curtains swaying, familiar, nor the manner in which the sunlight slants through the openings between them.

Slowly, I turn my head towards the light, willing my brain to interpret what my eyes are envisaging, willing it to tell me that I am not still dreaming.

He lies on his stomach, head buried beneath the pillow, his arms above his head. His bare back heaves slightly as he breathes, with the calm comfort of those soundly asleep. His hair is a mess of dark curls, sharply contrasted against the off-white duvet.

Memories rush back from the void, and I feel my cheeks burning.

I can't believe I did that. Swallowing, I mentally correct myself. *Well, to be precise, that* we *did* that.

For a moment, I panic, thinking this will be detrimental to my professional image, but there is no one else here. Everyone at the

Italian affiliate is at home with their families, and my own colleagues are all back in London. Besides, it is not as if I have been involved with a co-worker, or a client.

Before I can stop myself, I lean on one elbow, reaching out to let my fingers gently trail his delicate spine. It is as though I need to assure myself he is real, and not an apparition, and for this sight and smell and hearing alone cannot be trusted.

He stirs, and with the sudden speed of a cobra, I snatch my hand away, watching in horror as he struggles to turn around, tangled in the sheet, detaching himself from the pillow. Scrunching his eyes up against the brightness of day, he runs a hand through his hair. Then his eyes seem to focus on me, and I realise my knuckles have turned as white as the sheet they are frantically grasping.

"Hey", he says softly, his voice slightly hoarse from sleep. He smiles, and I feel myself relax. "Sleep well?"

"Very well", I say, daring to lean back down against the pillows. "You?"

"Like the dead", he chuckles, rubbing his eyes. "As you could probably tell." He leans over to the bedside table, checking his watch. I realise I have no idea what time it is, and it should be worrying me far more than it does.

"You don't have anywhere specific to be today, do you?" he asks, his tone casual, his eyebrow raised. I raise mine in return.

"What are you thinking?" He shrugs.

"Nah, nothing special. Just thought we could do a little tour."

Do I have somewhere specific to be? Well, obviously, seeing as I am here for work. The site inspection might be done, and it is mostly up to me to finish the report in my own time, but as I am here, I should probably sit in on the department meeting. Then again…

"Let me just make a phone call", I say. "I might have to listen in on a meeting, but I can tell them I ate something bad last night and will not come to the office. Then we can leave as soon as it is done. Would that be alright?"

"Alright", he says, seemingly amused as he brushes my hair over my shoulder, his thumb gently gracing my cheek. "Don't be too long."

"I won't", I promise, kissing his cheek in return, already wishing I could simply ignore what little morals I apparently have completely.

I should have begun to realise that our perspectives on what constitutes "a little tour" are somewhat contrasting, yet I somehow do not think further of it until we approach the docks, and he draws the attention of a crew member atop deck of a large white catamaran by whistling and waving his arm.

"What time do you set out?"

"Another half hour", he replies, hauling a rope over his shoulder. The sun is already burning on our backs, the morning bright and clear, the scents of the port drifting on a light breeze that sweeps my hair in an auburn torrent around my head.

"Tickets on the boat?"

"*Si.*"

"Where are we going?" I whisper as we step across the gangplank, the clang of our feet on metal unnaturally loud in the stillness of the port. He points out to sea.

"You know what's on the other side?" I laugh, convinced he's joking.

"What, Croatia?"

"That's where we're going."

"Seriously?" I glance around. "We're just going to skip country for a day? Who are you?"

He only grins, broadly, performing a mock bow like an on-stage magician. I am still bewildered.

"Do I need my passport or something?" He sniggers.

"Relax, we're all in the European Union here."

"Well, some of us are not anymore, as you may recall", I say, rolling my eyes. He nudges my shoulder.

"Still let you guys into the Euros though, eh?" he says, and I suppress a snort.

"We didn't defect from Europe, last time I checked. I mean, Iceland is not in the EU either and they got to play. As we learnt, the hard way." I pull a face and he laughs, dropping a gentle kiss on the side of my neck. The gesture is so simple, so natural, and I have no clue what to do, how to react.

We walk over to the cafeteria to buy coffee, and, realising we accidentally bypassed the massive breakfast buffet, something to eat. Nico waves my wallet away, talking to the older man behind the counter, who nods, seemingly understanding even if he struggles somewhat to respond.

"*Si...due panini.*" He busies himself with the cutting board, the knife, the fresh cheese and dried ham that seem far too fine for a simple ferry kiosk. "*Uno momento.*"

And then, sensing the other man's broken Italian, Nico switches, just like that.

"Je li u redu platiti karticom?" Is it okay to pay by card?

The other man lights up, his gestures broader now, talking as if to an old friend.

"*Da, da. Hvala.*" He hands over our food, smiling. "*Lijepo vrijeme danas. Uživaj!*" *Nice weather today. Enjoy!*

"You're full of surprises", I say as we settle on deck, our backs to the sun and watching the port of Ancona recede in the distance. He shrugs, though I can tell he is pleased by the way that smile plays at the corner of his mouth.

"My grandmother was Croatian", he says. "Met my grandfather during the war. I used to spend summers there. After all, it's not that far away, and we do have many things in common. The love of good food, for one."

"And multilingualism, clearly."

"Nah, come on. It's just courtesy. Down here, if you live close to a border – any border – it's more or less mandatory." He gives a shrug as he chews his sandwich. "Nothing strange."

Suddenly, I feel silly. I am the one with the long education, all the fancy academic titles, and yet all I have is my native English. And here he is, trotting out language after language like biscuits at high tea.

"Anyway, want to tell me about where we are going?"

"You'll see. But I can tell you it will be worth it, especially on a clear day like this. They say Zadar has the most beautiful sunset in the world. At least Hitchcock thought so." I arch an eyebrow.

"That's quite a statement. Can it live up to it, I wonder?"

"Judge for yourself. I doubt you'll be disappointed." He winks. "If you are, the next tour is on you."

After hours on the dazzling blue surface of the Adriatic, I have a vision that many a sailor, once upon a time, must have been bent over with relief to be faced with – dark shadows that gradually develop into rolling hills. The closer we get, the more rugged they appear, an untamed landscape without sign of human interference.

"This is the Kornati National Park", Nico explains as the ferry navigates a narrow straight between two islands, flanked by rocks and covered by low, thick vegetation. "George Bernard Shaw once famously claimed it to be the crowning of creation. There are hundreds – thousands – of islands along this coast, and some of the more secluded are here, outside of Zadar. They have some of the most amazing beaches that you can only reach by boat, and there are plenty of secret caves and little coves. During the war, ships used to hide here, in specially built tunnels drilled into the rock."

"You are quite the tourist guide", I say, smiling, marvelling at this unexpected side of him.

"Every place has its own history. You shouldn't just visit; you need to experience it. Understand its culture, its people."

Despite its size, the ferry navigates deftly between rocks and skerries, skimming the shorelines of white pebbles. Sailboats and smaller motorboats float on the surf, provisionally anchored as a group of older children snorkel and dive around what appears to be a shipwreck, visible in its entirety from above, despite the depth.

"Oh wow", I breathe, leaning over the rail as we glide by. "It feels like I could almost reach the bottom from here!" The water is unimaginably clear, a bright, green-tinged turquoise that scarcely seems to be real. Mesmerised, I trace the intended route of the ferry, through the labyrinth of islets.

"Have you been here before?" he wonders, as the city slowly comes into view, brick-red rooftops and white stone reflecting in the glittering surface of the breathtakingly blue ocean.

"Never here", I say, my eyes scanning the horizon, drifting to the mountains visible beyond the edge of town, thin wisps of cloud clinging to the peaks. "I've been to Split once, though, with my brother." I smile, apologetically. "For a game, initially – Mike used to play, though not quite at your level, and now he has this thing about visiting all the historic arenas of Europe – but we made it into a long weekend. It was fun."

"A game, at Poljud?" He raises an eyebrow. "You're crazier than I thought."

"What do you mean?" I frown. "It's just a stadium."

"It's Poljud", he says, with a shrug. "It was absolute mayhem, wasn't it?"

"It was absolute mayhem", I concur, the imagery still vivid in my mind. The hour-long queue outside the stadium, the throng of bodies rallying to get through, the bright red flares, the old nationalistic songs echoing into the night. "But I loved it. The sense of unity, the passion they had for their team. That's what makes this sport so special."

"Even more special, for them." There is a thoughtful expression on his face. "Most people fight to earn the right to represent their country, to carry their flag, but they had to fight for the flag itself before they even got to that point. They're a young nation, but with a long history, and a proud people." I lean back, regarding him.

"You admire them."

"I do", he says, running a hand through his hair as the ferry slows to a halt, the foghorn announcing arrival. "They're a strong team, difficult to play against. Always fight their hearts out, no matter the score."

"Given the choice, would you rather have played for them or for Italy?" I let the teasing smile linger even as he shoves me, playfully, aside.

"My family claim is a bit far-fetched", he says, "and would make little sense – I am born and raised an Italian, and so are my parents. But I am proud of my history, my connection to this place." He bites his lip, and for a moment a flash of melancholy darkens his features, before he turns to me, brightening. "And I look very much forward to showing it to you."

We embark at the mouth of a narrow harbour, setting foot on a bustling yet not particularly crowded promenade. The stone walls of the old town rise before us, encapsulating the tiny peninsula as if to separate it from the more modern part of town in time as well as space. A quadrangular bell tower rises above our heads as we enter through a vaulted gate, cobbled streets twisting around vibrantly coloured houses. Somehow, the sun shines even more brightly here, throwing long shadows before us on the white stone, impossibly slim and distorted, like Giacometti figurines. Eventually, the street opens to a central square, the bell tower reaching for the cloudless sky above.

"Do you want to go up?" Nico asks, indicating with his thumb. "The view is lovely."

We climb the narrow stairs in a spiral, round and round without perception of height. The sound of seagulls calling slips through tiny cracks in the walls, not wide enough to qualify as proper windows. Finally, I duck my head beneath a low doorway and step back out into the light, the entire town of Zadar spread before me as an intricate miniature of narrow streets, embraced on three sides by the ocean.

The main square is surprisingly green, with a large lawn fringed by trees and dotted with remains of Roman columns. Market stands flank the walkway to the waterfront, selling everything from painted shells to football jerseys to rakija glasses emblazoned with the Croatian flag.

"Which way?" I ask as we reach the sea, its sparkling blue even brighter up close than from the deck of the ferry. On the horizon, the islands of the national park huddle like the backs of ancient sea creatures risen from the depths.

"Come here, you'll love this", Nico says, and I follow him along the pier, towards the edge of town, where broad stairs are unevenly, yet seamlessly, built into the quay. As the sea heaves, water flows back and forth across the lowest flights, drenching the feet of the pedestrians having stopped to rest and seep up the sunshine.

"This is called the Sea Organ", Nico says. "My grandmother used to bring me here when I was younger. Although she, and many of the locals with her, was quite sceptical before it was unveiled, she ended up being very proud of it. She used to say it is the music of the ocean, made comprehensible to human ears." He smiles, and there is both affection and sadness in his smile. He gestures to the stairs. "There are giant tubes beneath here, like in an organ, and when water flows in, it creates a sound that is unique for every wave, every movement of water."

I close my eyes, and absorb the sound, rising and falling in bursts as the waves ebb and flow. It lacks the depth and the drama of a normal organ, the sounds emerging from the pipes more resemblant of flutes, soothing, yet playful and alluring.

"I've never seen – or heard – anything like this before. What an extraordinary idea."

After a while, we sit down at a restaurant close to the quayside, floor-to-ceiling glass windows thrown open to let the pleasantly warm late summer air flood the terrace. The waiter gestures to the wine list and offers his recommendations; the white tastes heavenly, its fresh, floral notes tinged with a faint minerality, almost like the hint of salt on the ocean breeze.

"It is called Pošip", he explains, "a local grape, indigenous to Dalmatia. This particular one is from a small winery right here in Zadar. It's located only fifteen minutes outside the city, in an old barrack that was once used by the Yugoslav national army."

"It's lovely", I say, gently swirling my glass, soaking up the sensation. I feel Nico's eyes on me and realise there must be a dreamy expression on my face, one that for all I know reminds him of something. Heat rushes to my cheeks and I turn back to the waiter. "Could we buy it somewhere?"

"It is a very small production", he says, shrugging. "I don't know how many bottles they have left. But I do have some in the cellar. If you want to, I can get one or two for you."

"Oh, that would be far too kind." I smile, and I notice Nico's smile too, out of the corner of my eye. "Can we put it on the same bill?"

"Well…" He hesitates, looking over his shoulder. His voice drops to a conspiratorial whisper. "We could, but then I would have to charge full restaurant price. If you pay cash, it will be cheaper." He winks, and I cannot suppress a laugh.

"Fair enough", I say, diving into my wallet. "I only have Euros, though?"

"*Nema problema*", he says, deftly making the bills disappear into his pocket. "I take care of it." He raises his head. "Everything good for you as well, sir?"

"*Nikad bolje*", he smiles, leaning back, his eyes trained on me. "Never better."

The waiter disappears to collect our contraband, and I raise my glass to Nico's in salute.

"So you like wine?" he asks, and I pull a face.

"Student hazard. You need it to survive, but you can't really afford it, so you work your way through all the cheap stuff and by the time you start liking it, you have also come to understand the economy of the real deal and eventually realise you need to get a proper education so your job can finance your habits." I shrug, and he laughs. "What about you?"

"My father's family has been winemakers for several generations." He looks almost apologetic. *Of course they are.* "My uncle runs the vineyard now. My father helps him out from time to time, on the logistic end. It is in the Beneventano region, if you know it?" When I reluctantly shake my head, he explains, "In Campania, not far from the Amalfi Coast. The main town is Benevento, northeast of Naples. It's a small vineyard, small production – we make red wine from the Aglianico grape and white from Falanghina. It covers the family's house needs but we also sell to local restaurants."

"I would love to try it sometime", I hear myself saying, and although I know that it is unreasonable, my chest still warms at the small smile I am rewarded with.

When the sun starts to set, we settle the bill and exit towards the edge of town, where we are met with an uninterrupted view of the sun setting between the distant islands. A sailboat glides serenely across the smooth surface of water, outlined as a black silhouette against the bright golden backdrop. The sky seems on fire, the colour of blood red and sunflower yellow and in between the bright orange of a burning flame. A small crowd has gathered at the edge of the open quayside square, all eyes on the glowing orb slowly descending into the ocean.

Even as the light recedes, a circle etched into the ground gradually comes to life, sparkling like lightning, multiple colours blazing across its surface. It makes me think of the part of the oceanic depths they call the twilight zone, where all kinds of mysterious creatures reside, their bodies transparent and shimmering with bioluminescence.

"It is beautiful", I whisper, breathless, as Nico comes to stand behind me. His nose brushes the back of my neck, hairs rising on end, and he places a gentle kiss on my shoulder as I lean against him.

"So are you."

It is overwhelming. Him, the sunset, being here, all of this. I cannot believe it is happening, even as I feel his breath on my skin and his arms around me.

"*Is this the real life?*" I murmur to myself. "*Is this just fantasy?*"

"*Caught in a landslide*", he joins in, humming softly, "*no escape from reality.*"

I turn my head around, looking in his eyes, the flecks of green so very bright now, in the final sharp rays of light.

"Really?" I say, grinning, but he just shakes his head, indicating towards the horizon, as if he does not wish for me to miss a single second of nature's magnificent display.

"*Open your eyes, look up to the skies and see...*"

"That's my favourite song", I say quietly. "I can't believe you know those lyrics."

"Everyone knows those lyrics", he says, but he sounds pleased. "And if not, they should. Did you know that 'scaramouche' is not just a nonsense word? It comes from the Italian *scaramuccia*, which was a character in Commedia dell'arte shows during the 17th century."

"No way", I say, my gaze still fixed on the sunset, as instructed, but I sneak my hand into his where they are clasped around my waist.

"No, truly. He was kind of, what do you say, a trickster character. Dressed in black, creating – and then somehow solving – all kinds of sticky situations. There was even an actor famous for playing this type of roles, Tiberio Fiorillo."

"Never heard of him."

"You wouldn't have, I suppose. But now you know." His smile is contagious. "Consider it today's cultural lesson."

It is strange. Last night was all about body and less about mind, which is unusual enough for me, but today is a completely different experience. Different, but in no way less intriguing.

"Hey." He smiles at me, ruefully, as if reading my silence, my mind. "I might not have all those years in university, but I do know some things." He winks, and this time I turn my head despite his protests, kissing him back.

Chapter 5

It is late, far too late, when we stumble back in through the hotel entrance.

"I have an early flight tomorrow", he says, stifling a yawn and looking regretfully at me. "Sorry for being a bore."

"Me too", I say, "so don't worry. But I had a lovely day." He smiles, his eyes dancing even in the dark.

"So did I, Sienna", he replies, and I find I love the way he says my name. "So did I."

He puts his arms around me, planting a kiss on my forehead. I lean into him, fatigued beyond belief but soaring on the inside. I never want to let go.

"Sweet dreams, *bella*."

I smile groggily, happiness swelling in my stomach even as weariness makes my brain foggy. I will be leaving for the airport in four hours, but as my head hits the pillow, sleep is the last thing on my mind.

I clutch the pillow over my face in denial as the alarm bell rings, feeling as I have only just closed my eyes. Head heavy, I get dressed, cramming everything into my carry-on bag, realising as I do that I will have to check it in, now that I have the bottle of wine. I smile at the memory of the waiter's under-the-table deal, the cash payment, and tuck the bottle in to rest between my blazers, snug in its paper bag.

As I step out into the corridor, running a hand through my hair in a feeble attempt at resolving the mess, I notice the door to the room at the far end is open. Perhaps he is just leaving. Perhaps we could even go to the airport together. Smiling, I walk the few steps to his room, barging through the doorway without even bothering to knock.

"Sleep well?" I call.

Nothing. The cry of a seagull drifts through the room, and I realise the door to the patio is open. I move through the room, noticing the unmade bed, the empty wardrobe.

"Nico?" I call, but there is no one outside. The sea heaves beneath me as I lean over the railing, boisterous and loud, as if distraught. The sky is still dark, with only a faint glimmer over the horizon heralding the eventual return of the light.

Behind me, there is a flush coming from the bathroom, and I all but run back inside, waiting for him to finish.

The door opens, and an elderly maid steps out, drying her hands on her apron, her greying hair tidied back by a scarf.

"Oh!" My hand flies up to cover my mouth. "I'm so sorry, I didn't mean…" I take a step back, my mind spinning.

"*Scusi*", the older woman says, apologetic. "*Non parlo inglese.*"

"No, no, it's fine, I'm sorry, I didn't mean to bother you…" I am rambling, but still find myself walking further into the room, as if this is all a joke and he is hiding somewhere at the back, waiting for me. A distant part of my brain reminds me I still have a flight to catch, but right now this is somehow far less important than the acute lack of a suitcase, of personal items spread across the room, of anything whatsoever signifying that another person has ever occupied this space.

"Nico?" I ask again, disbelievingly, pathetically, as if my voice had the power to make him materialise at will. "Are you there?" My stomach sinks with every step, a black hole of emptiness opening inside, pulling everything brutally apart.

He left. He's gone.

I wonder, briefly, what I had expected, what claims I could possibly have made, what would have entitled me to presume he would wait for me. Yet it hurts, the brief, sharp stab of a wasp sting before it rapidly worsens, growing dull and insistent, a throbbing ache deep within your blood. It is an open wound, growing inside me, the rift widening by the second, as if the realisation is still struggling to catch up.

He's gone. Gone gone gone.

"*Non c'è nessuno qui*", the old lady says, gruffly, visibly annoyed at my prolonged presence and the unwelcome disturbance in her morning routine. I do not fully grasp all the words, but I do get her point. *There is no one here.*

I turn around in the doorway, one last time, as if there are answers it still may hold, secrets it has yet to reveal. Although I sense I have explored its every corner, there is nothing left but the scent lingering in the air. A faint trace of citrus, an intriguing hint of cedar, sandalwood – warm, aromatic, charismatic. Its essence is fleeting, like a dream rapidly fading, yet distinct enough to make a memory.

Chapter 6

"Oh. My. God."

Rachel perfectly manifests every cartoon where someone's jaw drops to their knees, which contrasts hilariously against her perfectly tailored presence. I never realised a state of complete shock could be thus accentuated by designer attire, but she looks exactly like I imagine a duchess who have just caught her maid committing an unthinkably indecent act on castle premises, and during work hours at that.

"Oh my God. Just… oh my God. You did WHAT?! You crazy woman. You, you…" She gestures. "Come on, we're going for a glass of wine. Or a bottle. Or two. Really, right now. And you're going to tell me EVERYTHING." I laugh.

"Rachel, you don't even know who he is!"

"Like that matters?" she scoffs. "Honey, he is an Italian professional footballer. What more do I need to know?"

We find two bar chairs at a hip joint just around the corner from Regent Street, the top seats in the house for observing the bartender's frenzied distribution of espresso martinis and large trays of oysters. There is something industrial about the lighting, dim and slightly tinged, which is fine – I am not certain I would be able to handle this conversation in broad daylight. Not even twelve hours have passed since I arrived back home and the lack of sleep is starting to make itself known, but Rachel insisted we still meet up for our weekly Friday cocktail and I find it is exactly what I need right now. Something about the empty, unkempt apartment seems particularly hollow today, and I have no wish to see it again tonight. At least not in a state of sobriety.

"So, was he boring to talk to? You know, all fit but totally dull, like those thugs that hang about at the gym? The 'biceps before brains' kind of type?" Rachel reaches for her gin and tonic and does not so much as glance at the waiter throwing appreciative looks at her curvaceous build. "God, that is delicious. Really, this is when a Friday properly morphs over into the weekend. These after work hours are precious things."

"Cheers to keeping traditions", I say, clinking my Margarita glass with hers.

"Now, back to the *matter at hand*", Rachel emphasises in her *let's get down to business*-voice. "Daft and dull?"

"Not at all." I am still surprised by the ease of our conversation, the fact that two so different worlds could collide and yet not clash. "He clearly comes from an educated family, though", I add. "Hardly your average street urchin-turned-pro."

"And he took you on a day trip. Across the Adriatic."

"With food, wine, walks around the old town, watching the sunset." I sip my drink. "Textbook stuff."

"You are incredible, do you know that?" Rachel sighs. "Who does this kind of thing? Of all people – you?! You barely pay attention to new people until they've been in the group for weeks, sometimes even months. It's like they're on a trial period. And now this?" I have to laugh.

"I do *not* put people on a trial period. I just need some time to get to know them, that's all."

"Huh." Rachel downs her drink and slides the empty glass across the counter, signalling for another. "Define 'some time'." The bartender, resting his tattooed arms on the bar, looks enquiringly at me. I have trouble deciding, yet it feels as though his eyes ask another question. *The time it takes*, I want to say, but I do not.

"Champagne", Rachel offers when I falter. "That always works."

"I don't feel much like celebrating, though", I sigh, but I accept the 1920's style flute nonetheless.

"We should all celebrate more", Rachel states, assuredly. "Your work meeting did go well, did it not? And you got a hell of a treat along the way."

"Well, yes."

"There you go." She takes a defiant sip of her fresh G&T. "You work too much, you know. That's your problem." I scoff.

"I do not! Or, sure, I work a lot, but that's what everyone with a career does, right?" I raise an eyebrow at her. "Like you don't work long hours too."

"I do", she says, slowly, carefully, as if weighing her words. "And it pisses me off every time, because I work to be able to afford all the other things I want to do, or have." She leans forward, eyeing me. "Of course I also want to do well, Sienna, same as you. But that does not mean putting my personal life on hold."

"I do not", I protest. "We do things. We hang out. Or doesn't that count?"

"I know you sit with your work computer open at 11 pm answering emails when we don't", she shoots back with a pointed look, and I cringe inwardly at how horrible it sounds. "Don't bother denying it. *That* is a problem."

"It's only when I have nothing better to do", I argue, but I can tell how feeble it comes out. "I am not going to burn out, or anything like that. Don't worry about me."

"That's not the point", Rachel says, exasperated. "Not everything is about your work performance. What about what *you* want, besides being successful? You don't actually *want* to spend the rest of your life reading work emails at night, do you?"

"It saves time for the next day", I shrug.

"To do what?" she bites back, and I know she has me there. "What do you do with all this time you save?"

Not enough, I think, but I hold back. She knows I am aware of this, but saying it out loud would still mean to acknowledge it. Make it real.

She answers in my stead, the way best friends do.

"You should try this new app. I had two clients in only this week who met through it, and they looked so ridiculously happy it would have made you throw up. Natalie who works in reception just started seeing a guy on there too."

"No, please", I groan. "Not another dating app. I can't take it, Rachel, I just can't."

"But this one is different", Rachel insists. "Look, they have all these…"

"They're all different", I cut her off, "yet the same." But she is unperturbed.

"I mean, as one-night stands go, you've already hit the jackpot. That's going to take a lot to beat. But I know you, Sienna. You want something stable. This is that kind of app."

"That might be, but it's the people on it that I worry about. You saw what happened with Nathan. One day he was saying how much he liked me and planning trips to visit his parents' house in Portugal and the next he was snogging some girl at a bar hopping event and posting it on Facebook for the world to see. People can't be trusted. *Men* can't be trusted."

I refrain from telling her how much more it took to come to terms Nico's empty hotel room than Nathan's betrayal, even though I am aware of the distorted perspective. How can I possibly feel more attached to someone I have just met, compared to someone I had been seeing for months?

He still left, remember? a nasty little voice inside me points out. *They all leave, eventually.*

"They all say they like 'strong women' but then it turns out they just don't want to be in a relationship with them." Luigi's comment about men not wanting to wait at home for their woman comes back to me, turning the champagne sour in my mouth. "Why is it always the woman who must choose between her partner and her career? Why not the man? Honestly, why should anyone?"

"Why are you always like this?" Rachel sighs. "You know I agree with you, by the way. But..."

"You know damn well why", I cut her off, and she nods, albeit reluctantly. I take a larger-than-polite gulp of my drink, using it to actively push the images from my mind. Yet they resurface, one by one. The muffled noises, the laughter, the creak of the door opening on rusty hinges. I feel sick.

"Still. You need to try, or you'll never know." Rachel fixates me with that sharp look of hers, and when she does, there are few who dare object.

My pocket buzzes the moment I step through the door of my depressingly dark flat, and I pull my phone out, expecting Rachel's usual '**Home safe**' message. Instead, I see my brother's number light up the screen.

F1 Sunday? the text from Mike reads.

I respond by giving him the thumbs up. We have not had one of those in a while, and I feel bad about missing races with so little of the season remaining. Our dad would not have approved; Sunday afternoons in front of the TV are as holy to him as the mornings are to diligent churchgoers.

Wine or beer? I offer, as it is usually me in charge of drinks, and Mike at the barbecue.

I'm feeling wine on this one. Red? It's Monza after all.

Indeed. The thought of Italy sends an uncontrollable shiver down my spine. *Not now, please.* I need to think of something else. Anything. I make a mental note to find some good Italian wine first thing in the morning. Mike likes Barolo, but suddenly I am itching to make him try something new, unexpected.

You got it. See you at 2!

Chapter 7

The walk up to Mike's house always manages to put a smile on my face, mostly because it, one, actually is rather pretty, given that the Docklands constitute one of the few areas in view of the Thames that can also boast to be in the vicinity of clear water, and two, because the Fraser Place apartments in Canary Wharf are so ridiculously flashy and my brother is so utterly unsnobbish, unless it happens to revolve around cars.

"It was one of the few places in town where I could park my car and no one would comment", was his standard phrase when asked about the location of choice, and it must have worked, given that he is still here. I gently run my hand over the smooth, well-polished – as always – hood of the bright green Porsche. Not many people are willing to spend about as much on their car as on their apartment, but Mike and I have always had a special relationship with vehicles. Our father, a retired mechanic and engineer with a once-upon-a-time podium finish in the Scotland Rally, was big on introducing us to engines of all sorts from the moment our legs were too long for the plastic toy car we kept pushing ourselves around on, back and forth in the corridor – much to our mother's dismay – and out into the garden. Growing up meant following him to race events, where he claimed he was 'working', though mostly we figured he was chatting up old mates or doing unofficial commentary for one of the local radio stations whose airwaves rarely reached beyond the local pub. By the time Mike was trying out for his driver's licence, we had already done the rounds in go-kart and quarter-midget racing and made each other a solemn sibling pact – we would, within the next fifteen years, be in possession of our dream cars. In retrospect, this was slightly unfair on me, as I was younger and my dream more expensive, but I still have not given up. Every time I renegotiate my salary, I envision the red lightning cruising along serpentine roads in distant mountains, and I make myself push it just a little more, even though I know it would probably have been easier if I had followed Mike's example and chosen finance. But I like science, and the sense of contributing to society; if I can do something useful and make money at the same time, I tell myself I can allow to postpone the dream a little longer.

The roast is already in full flow on the balcony when I step through the doorway, delicious vestiges of rosemary, ground black pepper and fresh thyme floating on the air. I stick my head around the corner, finding my brother in his best apron, a pair of pliers in one hand and a cutting-board of marinated lamb racks in the other.

"Greetings, chef", I say, making him turn and crack a smile. Though we do not look particularly much alike, we have the same blue eyes, faint traces of white running through the iris the way newly fractured ice criss-crosses a mountain lake in the spring, and the same chestnut hair, mine long and flowing, his short and unruly, never remaining in the same position for long.

"Si!" He puts the meat down and pulls me into a hug, which I return while simultaneously trying to avoid being skewered on the pliers. "Good to have you home." He drops a kiss on the top of my head, privilege of the tall, and nods to the bag I am carrying. "Spill it. I'm getting thirsty working hard on this excellent lamb over here."

I reach into the bag and pull out the bottle I brought, smiling triumphantly as I do.

"Aglianico", Mike reads, and I feel a momentary stab in my chest. I told myself I would not go looking for anything to do with him, but when I asked for recommendations 'off the beaten track', well…

"They refer to it as the 'Barolo of the south'", I repeat the salesman's words. "It's supposed to be great with meat."

"Neat", Mike says, still reading the label. "Crack it open and let's see if it delivers. The food is all but done. Mind checking on the potatoes in the oven?"

I set the table as Mike sets up his gargantuan TV to show the first warm-up laps already being run, the whistling sound of unimaginably powerful engines filling the apartment. I pour us wine, sniffing the rustic tones of tobacco and dark berries.

"Mmm", Mike quips, already a sip down. "This is it. Absolutely perfect."

He gets to work on serving, and I lose myself in the cars zipping round the track, the meditative noise, the speaker voice narrating the current standings of the championship, the starting line-up, who is in pole position and who messed up during the qualifiers, earning themselves a minute penalty and therefore banishment to the far back of the field. The camera sweeps over the pits, the bright red of Ferrari and the sleek dark silver of Mercedes easily recognisable among the other teams' motley composition of colours and sponsor logos. The panoramic view over the stadium continues, passing over the stands, which are full almost to the brim, flags fluttering in the wind and spirits seemingly high.

Suddenly, an all-too-familiar face shows up in the second row, and my ears abruptly tune in to the commentator's voice, as if finally finding the correct frequency on an erratic radio:

"…and they certainly have prominent support today in AC Milan midfielder Nicolo Di Luca and fellow defender Federico Rossi…"

I choke on my wine. The cough racks my body so hard I think my ribs might crack, and Mike shoots me a look.

"You okay?" he asks tentatively, eyebrow raised.

"I'm fine", I croak hoarsely, my eyes still on the TV, the camera trailing the two men hiding – moderately successfully – beneath red Scuderia Ferrari caps. *Oh God he is a Ferrari fan, isn't he? He just had to be. Although he's Italian, so I suppose he couldn't be anything else, or he'd lose his passport.*

"Sis, what's going on? You look like you've seen a ghost."

No, I just saw a man I've slept with on TV. While I usually tell my brother everything, there is no way I can tell him about this. I swallow.

"Sorry", I say. "I... forgot to tell you something." I smile my sweetest and most innocent smile, which in all honesty is not that sweet and innocent at all. "I saw him this week. When I was in Italy for work."

"What? Who?" I point to the screen.

"Di Luca." *God, it feels strange now, to think of him by his last name.* "He was at my hotel."

"No way." Mike turns around in his seat, fully facing me. He knows that I am not a liar, but I can tell he is struggling to wrap his mind around this one. To be entirely fair, so am I. Still, I nod.

"Yeah, I got him to sign my calendar and we chatted a bit." An image of a lean body beneath a stream of water flashes before my eyes, and I bite my tongue. "So weird but totally worth it."

"Si, what the hell." Mike shakes his head, incredulous. "Can I see?"

"See what?"

"Your calendar, wiseass. Where he signed?"

"Oh, yeah." I reach for my bag and fish it out, handing it over open to the first page. He takes it, almost reverently, smoothing down the pages as if attempting to assess by sight alone whether it is genuine.

"Si..." He lets out a low whistle as he hands it back. "And you didn't think of telling me about this?"

"Sorry, I really just forgot, honestly." I smile, hoping it comes across as real. "I guess I was still a bit overwhelmed." *No lies there.*

“He seems like a really nice guy.” *Who incidentally left without saying goodbye.*

We sit in silence for a moment, absorbing the screeching of tires on asphalt.

“So what are you up to this week?”

“Not much.” I shrug. “Writing up internal reports and following up on the site visit is going to take up most of my time. Got a happy hour thing with some old lab mates on Thursday and I haven’t found a good reason to say no yet. Maybe I should just go this time, I haven’t seen them in ages.”

“You should definitely go”, Mike affirms. “You need to get out more.”

“Not you too”, I say, giving him a friendly shove. “Rachel is on my case all the time.”

“She’s right, you know. How is she?”

“Good. Busy. But happy, I think. Annoyed at her clients, as usual. Annoyingly in love with Tom, still.”

“They’ve been married, what? Two years now?”

“And together for twelve. It’s quite amazing, if you ask me. I can’t seem to put up with people – or they with me – for even two months.”

“Well, I guess that’s a family trait.” He shrugs, and I know he’s not just referring to us. There are plenty of single households in every generation.

“You’re too good for these stock market groupies anyway”, I say, leaning back against the sofa. “If you ever let one of them drive that car, I will maim you.” He laughs, and we clink our glasses together.

“To chasing dreams”, he says, “and always being in the driver’s seat.”

I salute him, even as I suddenly wonder whether my dream should encompass something more, something else.

Someone else, in the passenger seat, as the sun blazes over the lacquer and everything else turns to dust behind us.

Chapter 8

Writing reports has never been my thing, and come Thursday it has become tedious enough to force me out of my reverie and make the trip across town to the designated den of the Carter lab, located along the Strand at a convenient walking distance from King's College. As I drag my steps from Temple station, I longingly cast a glance up at the Radio rooftop bar, which is more my cup of tea – or tailor-made cocktail, if you will –, but force myself to keep walking until I reach the unflatteringly brown entrance to The Wellington. The tables outside on the street are full, despite the chill on the air and the arm's length at which a steady stream of cabs pass by, heading for the theatre district. I wave my hand through the plumes of cigarette smoke, holding back the urge to cough pointedly.

The pub is shaded in half-light, the kind that hides the cracks in the floor and the stains on the tables that will not wash away. A girl shoulders her way through the crowd, bumping into me as she balances multiple pints of beer in both of her hands. It is packed, rowdy, and utterly British.

"Sienna! Over here!"

A waving hand down at the back, and I gesture towards the bar in return, indicating that I will get myself a drink first, even though a small part of me would rather instinctively bolt for the door. Instead, I reluctantly make my way over, sipping my rather bland and far too warm wine as I say my hellos, taking in the familiar faces.

"...and then I had to redo *all* my experiments", Eleni sighs theatrically, "just because Reviewer 2 claimed they could not take the data points seriously if there were two outliers. I mean, what were we supposed to do? We couldn't very well *exclude* them, could we?"

"Reviewer 2 is always a bitch", Sean, with whom I used to share an office, says sympathetically. "It's like the professors' version of the 'good cop-bad cop' thing – one is so overly positive you get suspicious; one evidently woke up and chose violence, and one has barely read the paper at all except for the part about their particular method of interest, which they are now taking apart into such minute detail they might discover the Higgs particle in there while they're at it." Eleni groans, hiding her face in her hands, and I cannot hold back a smile.

"Hi guys", I say, dropping down into the seat next to Sean, giving him a quick hug. "Good to see you. Some journal giving you trouble?"

"The usual", Sean supplies. Glancing over at Eleni, he adds, in a lower note, "I still reckon they'll take it, though. She'll just have to bust her ass in the coming weeks, and she obviously isn't thrilled about it." He runs a hand through his mop of messy red hair. I try to calculate how long time he has left before he is finished, but I know I cannot ask. That is one of the unspoken rules of grad school; to most students, the defence date is uncannily similar to the pot of gold at the end of the rainbow – it never seems to get any closer. I still remember the shock on their faces when I told them I was going to be done and leaving within the designated three years, as if that was not the entire intention of the programme.

"Hey, where is Laura?" I ask, looking around. "Wasn't she coming?" My former lab mate used to be a regular at these things, more often than not organising the entire event. She had the experience, after all, having been around already when I arrived and still there when I left.

"About to give birth any minute, last I heard", Michelle drawls in her Canadian accent, her uncut strawberry blonde hair tumbling messily over the table as she leans on her elbow. "So I guess we're hardly her first priority." I can feel my eyes bulging.

"She's pregnant? Since when?"

"Since about nine months", Sean supplies helpfully. "That's usually how it goes."

"Well, yeah, obviously, but..." I shake my head. *When did I last take the time to really catch up with these people? How much have I missed since I left?* "I didn't even know she had a boyfriend." *Or that she would ever be able to give up drinking, even if only temporarily.*

"By the way, Sean, whatever happened to that girl you were seeing?"

"Bah, didn't work out. Conversing with a wall would have been less dull. She didn't even know how to do an ELISA properly. Honestly, I'm absolutely *amazed* she managed to get a grad student position." He rolls his eyes and takes a swig of beer. "Her committee is going to have a field day with that one, I tell you. Pipetting error is an understatement, and I'm being nice."

"I'm a whiz at ELISAs, you can go out with me", a voice from the far end of the table pipes up. "Did fourteen plates in one go last night. Masterclass, that. Ready for *CSI: Miami*."

"Thanks for the offer, Pedro, but I'm afraid you're not really my type", Sean calls back. "No offense, it's just something about the beard. It's not you, it's me, I promise."

These geeks, I think to myself, both fondly and somewhat sadly at the same time. The thought of Rachel's app comes to my mind, unbidden. *Is that the only option, to not end up like this?* I curse inwardly, caught between the devil and the deep blue sea.

"I've never seen them do ELISAs on *CSI*", Michelle says, frowning as she pulls at the frizzy ends of her hair. Thin, pale, sad-looking strands pile up on the greasy table next to her. I silently wonder how many times I have seen her put off a haircut until it is inevitable in order to make her rent.

"They do all kinds of random laboratory methods on these shows", Pedro assures her. "Anything normal people have no idea of and therefore believe to be fancy and advanced and complex, while we know that in fact it is first, simple routine that could be managed by a monkey, and second, absolutely the wrong choice of method for the question they're asking. All you have do is look good doing it."

"Well, that certainly rules you out then, doesn't it?" Sean quips. "Given what your wardrobe looks like, getting you decent styling would effectively blow their budget out of the water."

Am I really that different? I ask myself even as I secretly roll my eyes at them. *Or do I just try so hard to be?*

I realise I have a role with these people, a role I am not certain I fill anymore. I feel like a fraud, listening in on these scientific conversations, these everyday scholarly struggles. A traitor, for leaving, an infiltrator who no longer talks about reviewers and impact factor and methods development as if they constituted the entire universe. I no longer need to worry about protocol modification when no protocol is available because the publication keeps referring to 'as previously described' and the original description happens to predate the Internet.

Is it I who have changed, or just they who have not? The liquor-sticky counter, the cheap beer on tap, the raucous bar crowd – all of them things I thought I had left behind at graduation. I was already on my way, forwards, onwards, upwards. Or so I thought.

"So, Si, how is industry?" Eleni asks, as if on cue, and suddenly, the mood changes, as if a mythical creature has taken up residence in their midst. The mere word 'industry' signifies change, an inexplicable otherworldly reality that might as well be removed from theirs by another dimension.

"It's okay", I say truthfully. "Lots of work, same as before. Just a different type of work." I shrug, refraining from adding it also pays more than twice the salary.

“Sorry for asking, but what is it that you actually do?” Eleni leans forward, and I see the faint hope in her eyes, the desperate belief that something better lies beyond the seemingly insurmountable obstacle of graduation. The same hope I used to feel, when I was rushing towards the finish line, too busy to stop and look why no one was following.

“Don’t you miss doing real research, though?” someone asks. Tess, I think her name is, an Irish girl in Pedro’s group. Brown-rimmed round spectacles, mousy hair, a backpack squeezed between her knees.

“For £80.000 a year, I wouldn’t miss it one bit either”, Pedro states, and laughter erupts as I roll my eyes, trying to wave it away.

“Not really”, I say, though this is not the whole truth. “I guess it varies from day to day. I don’t miss the experiments, or the late nights… But sometimes I do miss the feeling of things coming together, of realising I made a connection no one else has made before.” I shrug.

I hate how defensive the ‘real research’ comment makes me. I do not need to justify anything – they all knew where I was heading, right from the start – but for some reason I still feel I do. Perhaps it is not so much my profession as my self-inflicted solitude. I might as well have joined a convent.

“Never happened to me anyway”, Sean says, getting up, “at least not sober. Hence: who wants more beer?”

That same evening, I log on to the app, foul words lining up in my brain as I fill in the required details.

This is stupid, I tell myself. *You need to get over it. It was a once-in-a-lifetime thing. You don’t even know the guy. It wouldn’t have worked anyway.*

How do you know, though? But I know better than to get into an argument with myself; that would most likely qualify for some form of uncomfortable diagnosis.

He left you, just like the others. Why do you even care?

I scroll though the silly prompts, asking you to list just about everything that is not useful to know about a person you have never met. **Two truths and a lie. As seen on my mum's fridge. A shower thought I recently had.** *Seriously?*

I keep scrolling, incredulous.

Did I mention that… I shake my head. What does that even mean? What do they expect me to write? *That I have too high standards?*

Fuck it, just write the truth. I snigger to myself as I enter **…that I hate online dating.**

Chapter 9

For reasons beyond the early hour, I feel utterly miserable as I trudge down the street to Limehouse station. It has been raining all night and this morning is no different, save for even deeper puddles by the sidewalks. The strap of my computer bag digs into my shoulder as I fight desperately with both hands to salvage my umbrella in the raging gusts of wind. To make matters worse, as I walk down the steps to the train, my phone beeps. I fumble with umbrella, bag, Oyster card and phone, in fear of dropping several or all of the above before I manage to look at the screen. My mother.

"Hello", I say tentatively as I draw to a halt, much to the annoyance of the onslaught of people around me, in the middle of the staircase. She hardly ever calls.

"Sienna, darling, how are you?" *Is she calling me to make small talk? At this time of day?* It is all I can do not to glance at my watch.

"Fine." Not really, but how will she be able to tell? "Has something happened? I thought you'd be at work at this hour."

"The morning meeting was cancelled, so I got to sleep in." She clears her throat, and I can tell all the way from Ipswich there is something she really does not want to tell me.

"Spill it, Mum", I say. "I'm about to get on a train and lose the signal."

"Martin and Evelyn are having a baby." The words come tumbling down the phone line with the speed of an oncoming avalanche, as if she is relieved to get rid of them. I feel my throat turn dry. For an instant, I sway on my feet as I stand. I should not care. It is none of my business. At least not anymore.

"Thanks for letting me know", I say, forcing my voice to remain as neutral as possible. Somehow, it being her to tell me makes it all even worse. I imagine the glee in her sister's voice as she broke the news. Despite not having spoken properly for years, this is apparently important – and humiliating – enough to warrant a breach in radio silence. "I've got to go, okay? I'll talk to you on Sunday."

Good for them, I tell myself as I wobble down the stairs. *This isn't the life you wanted, anyway.* Yet, below it all, there is a sensation I recognise, and genuinely despise. Of being left out, cast aside, deceived and replaced.

The tube is cramped, the windows misting over from the condensed damp air of hundreds of people huddling together in jackets that are either too thin for the outdoors or too thick for the underground. I squeeze myself into a corner, shutting my eyes against the glumness of the weather and my own dreary mood, but the dark thoughts still seep through.

At the office, I stare at my computer, but the numbers and tables refuse to make sense. I despise the way I cannot seem to focus on anything else but the mirages rolling through my mind, over and over, like an old VHS tape that you have tried to rewind and now is stuck on repeat. Sunlight through white curtains dotted with flowers, the pillowcases I had made in school, the photographs proudly mounted in frames along the bookshelves.

"Hey, Sonia", I call to our new assistant as she passes by, more to distract myself than anything else. "Where are we on the contract with Dr Stevens for his upcoming lecture?"

"I'm not sure that's my responsibility?" she says, raising a well-groomed eyebrow. "I am working on the patient education programme; I have my plate full already."

"Sonia." I lean forward over my screen, keeping my voice level. "You are responsible for Medical Affairs contracting. That means *all* our contracts, whether for lectures, patient support, advisory boards, or any form of consulting, for any purpose. I am fully aware this is quite a handful; if you need help prioritising, come to me and I will be glad to sort you out." I clasp my hands together over my keyboard. "Now, the lecture takes place ten days from now at a major national conference. Dr Stevens is highly respected in the community and a valued collaborator, and we would prefer it stays that way. We therefore need the invitation distributed as soon as possible, but we cannot do that unless the contracting process is completed, which makes this first priority."

"Yes, but..."

"Sonia, the patient education series is not set to start until after New Year's. We do not even have a venue confirmed. It can wait." Sonia purses her lips, her displeasure palpable, but I am undeterred. "Is that clear?"

There is a moment of tense silence, then she nods, briefly, before turning her back on me without another word. Her heels tap the floor aggressively. With a heavy sigh, I rest my forehead against my desk and reach for my phone.

Friday drinks at my place tonight? I text Rachel. **Stay out of the rain? It feels like a 'bottles rather than glasses' kind of day.**

"Have you met anyone yet?" Rachel prompts as soon as she flops down on my sofa, kicking off her shoes and putting her feet up on the low stone table, sighing audibly. "Christ, what a week. I feel like a wet rag someone wrung out and left to dry, only for it to get soaked again in the next rain shower."

I look out the window; it is still raining. Representative, British fall drizzle against a solid grey backdrop. I actively wish myself away to warmer climates and bluer skies as her words, on top of everything else, force me to think back on the farce of the past few weeks' presence on the fabled app, which, to be frank, most of the time makes me want to bang my head against a wall.

"Let's see, where should I start? With the guy with the blue ponytail or the one whose dream vacation spot was Chernobyl?"

"Gosh, you're hopeless. Skip the freak show and tell me the good bits. Anyone who seems legit?"

I sit down next to her on the sofa, handing her a glass of chilled Chablis. She pulls her head up from the armrest and takes a large, unsophisticated gulp. "God, that's good. Exactly what I needed. You're the best."

I offer her a half-smile, my thoughts already drifting, unintentionally leading me back to last week's miseries. The first one was somewhat younger than me, not by much, two-three years at the most, working in IT. Friendly enough, until the conclusion of the bill. Re-enacting the moment he sees the number on the slip of paper, I do not know whether to laugh or cry.

"Perhaps you can take the bill?" he says, looking nervous. "And then I can wire you the money?"

I blink. *Wow, that's a whole new level of 'Thanks for dinner but I already know I'll never see you again'. Or is this just what happens after thirty when you try to engage with kids who spend their whole lives behind computer screens?*

The second one could have passed for an obscure post-doc in my old lab, shuffling from bench to bench, his large round spectacles sliding down his nose as he bends over a microscope. Except in this case, a drinks menu, which he scrutinises with minutiae detail. His blond hair is cropped short, except for some escapee curls that he does not seem to notice. I scrutinise my wine glass, waiting.

"The Syrah is really good", I offer, after what approaches ten minutes of intense silence.

"I don't really like wine", he shrugs. "But I'll have a cocktail."

"Sure", I say, twirling my glass and feeling I should perhaps have let him order first, and followed suit.

"You see, I have this cocktail cupboard at home…" He leans over, showing me on his phone. As he swipes between photos, I am treated to all imaginable angles of a dark wooden monstrosity, with ornate iron keys in the locks of polished doors inlaid with patterns of clinging vines and stylised nymphs. On the inside, glasses are lined up with millimetre exactness in an obsessive-compulsive fashion, and there is a separate section for each type of liquor. He has more pictures of that cupboard than most mothers have of their new-born babies. I shift in my chair.

"And then", he proceeds, oblivious, "the plan is to..."

"I'll stop you right there", I say, smiling to take the edge off my words, which are bordering on panic. "It looks amazing. How about expanding it with a bar counter so you can mix drinks properly as well? I would have guessed that was the point of all these spirits."

"Oh, I never really thought about that." He shrugs. "They're good in themselves, but mostly I kind of just like to watch it, you know? Feel that *Great Gatsby* vibe coming off it."

Back in the safety of the present and my flat, I take another sip of Chablis and throw my best friend a pointed look.

"Seriously? His cocktail cupboard?" Rachel groans. "Why do you always go out with the weird ones?"

"Because either they're all like that, which indeed is quite possible, or they just happen to be the only ones who will go out with me", I shoot back. "It's you who keep insisting I should try my way, so make up your mind."

"Well, yes, but you might need to work on some form of selection process."

"Why bother? It never lasts anyway."

"It doesn't last because you don't allow it to. You don't trust them." Rachel's expression is accusing, but I can only shrug.

"I don't trust them because they give me no reason to. Speaking of nothing, do you remember Sean?"

"Sean from your lab group? The ginger one, who is always cracking jokes?" Rachel asks. "What about him?"

"I saw them last week, the whole gang. I just can't stop thinking about that he ought to be finishing soon. He's a smart guy and he started around the same time as me. I don't understand why he keeps taking so long to wrap things up."

"Maybe he's happy where he is?"

"Oh, come on." I all but roll my eyes. "Academia is a stepping-stone, not a permanent solution. The entire point of the exercise is to get out."

"For you, yes. Everyone else might not see it that way. Remember those people who hung around at uni forever? They would finish one course and then move on to the next one, even though the topics might be completely unrelated. Like they just couldn't let go of that life."

"True." I wonder, suddenly, whether I would have felt differently about it, had the circumstances been different. *Another thing I will never know.*

"Hey", Rachel says, leaning forward, staring at me intently. "You and Sean. Wouldn't that be a thing?"

"No", I scoff, yet even as I do, an insistent memory rises to the surface, of Christmas lights and homemade liquor brewed in conical lab flasks, of fading music and a corridor leading to the kitchen, narrow enough for two less-than-sober individuals passing simultaneously to physically bump into each other. "I like Sean, I really do. Always have. But… no. Not like that." Rachel sighs dramatically.

"Well, no one can say I didn't try. Perhaps you just need some time off. You know, go away, mull over what you want."

"I don't need to go on vacation to 'find myself'. I'm fine on my own, you know. And people don't actually do that, do they? It's just something that sounds good, going away and hoping all your troubles will solve themselves while you're relaxing by the pool."

"On the contrary, they do", Rachel says. "Except you, who never take vacation."

Apparently, I find out things about myself on my work trips instead, I think bitterly. *And lose them, equally fast.*

"Enough about me", I say instead. "Can't we talk about your problems? Because I do suppose you still have them, even though your life is mostly annoyingly perfect."

"Ha!" Rachel snorts. "You wish. But you're right, there are things we could talk about. Have you ever had to fire anyone? Asking for a friend."

Sonia's sour expression immediately pops into my head, and I wince. She has only been with the company for a couple of months, but her attitude is already that of a grumpy old lady who is sticking it out until retirement, keeping to the bare minimum.

"No, I can't say that I have", I say, slowly going over the comings and goings in my vicinity at work. "The people I manage… I don't have the final say, but I can give – or not give – recommendations, and then my boss is the one who makes staffing decisions. Why?"

"A certain amount of, how shall I put it, *misconduct*, has been observed." Rachel sounds uncomfortable. "When Natalie came in the other day she found the other receptionist, Sophie, together with one of the clients who had booked a meeting that morning. Except, well…"

"…they weren't really discussing furniture", I fill in, grimacing. "That's gross."

"To my knowledge, they actually could have been", Rachel objects. "Especially their alternative uses."

"Eww, Rachel, spare me the details. Alright, so you will have to fire her, that's pretty obvious. Why do you need my opinion?"

"Well, the thing is, they are about to pay us loads of money. I mean *loads*. His shopping list is bordering on the obscene. If I fire her now, he might get upset and pull out. If I don't and this comes out, it's going to look really bad for me for keeping her on. And regardless I will have to speak to Natalie and explain, so there is no way this will remain a managerial secret for long."

"Shit." I let out a slow whistle. "I hear you." Reaching for the bottle, I top up her glass. "Can't you talk to her? Sophie, I mean? Make sure she secures the deal, the client is happy, and then you give her some form of garden leave package to walk quietly, no questions asked. Under the circumstances, I think that's your best bet. Natalie would never stay on if Sophie was allowed to, and I assume you'll want to keep her." Rachel nods, thoughtfully.

"You know, all those degrees. You might actually have acquired some analytical skills", she says. "Who knew?"

She ducks as the pillow comes flying at her, but not fast enough.

I spend Sunday night watching Serie A, almost by chance as I turn on the TV while ironing laundry. Milan are playing Fiorentina, and unsurprisingly, I find Nico's name in the starting line-up. I know I should probably turn the thing off, but both my hands are busy, and by the time the players run out onto the pitch, it is already too late. While I am prepared this time, I am still overcome by a similar sense of surrealism as when watching the Monza Grand Prix with Mike. Seeing him like this, in his natural element, is what I am used to. He has always been an image on the other side of a screen, recognisable, yet untouchable, a two-dimensional rendition of a real being. Before, I would have been engrossed in the game, already following his movements with particular interest, but now, I find another facet has been added. As the match unfolds, I repeatedly catch myself reading his face, seeking to interpret his thoughts and emotions, the nuances in how he reacts to a controversial call or a teammate misplacing a pass. At the end, the ironing board stowed away and a cup of coffee in my hands, I am as transfixed as I have ever been. It is not his best game, which is hardly to be expected, this early in the season and so close after the international break, but his technique remains flawless, and he constantly manages to put his teammates into positions from where they have a chance to score. In the end, they do, a header following a lovely, floating cross, and I almost yell in celebration.

What are you doing? a voice inside me pleads. *He left. You owe him nothing.*

My phone buzzes, and absently, as if my subconscious is willing me to distance myself from the man on TV, I flip open the cursed app to find a new like.

He left. Don't do this to yourself. It is almost a mantra at this point.

You can say that again, is the reply to me hating on online dating. That alone makes me snigger.

John, his name is, and judging from the pictures, he has a nice smile. In one he is cradling a magnum bottle of wine the way one would a baby; in another, he is in Pisa, putting his hand out nonchalantly to 'support' the leaning tower. It is a pose I have seen hundreds of times before, but something about the goofy look on his face tells me at least he has a sense of humour.

Horrific, I write back. **You should see the specimens I've encountered already.**

Not sure I want to know, if they're anything like their female counterparts. I kind of like women with brains.

Really? That's a first. I thought interesting conversation was a lost art form.

Judging from the way he writes, he seems decent. From his education and one of the more professional-looking photos, in a pinstriped shirt and navy suit, fully attired with a brown leather briefcase, I gather he must be in law, or at least something along these lines.

Hey, he finally types. **Call me old-fashioned, but this chatroom vibe doesn't really do it for me. Want to meet?**

Chapter 10

We convene at a wine bar at the corner behind the Liberty warehouse, unpretentious wooden tables and high red metal chairs set against white-painted walls and bookshelves filled with bottles, utilising the warm oak from used wine cartons. *Antidote* the sign fittingly reads; I hear corks being pulled left and right as I make my way through the maze of bar tables and people curing their various ills.

I spot him sitting over by the window facing the street, watching the passers-by with interest, and stop to observe for a moment before making myself known. He has an open, friendly face, the type who always seems close to a smile. His hair is wavy, seemingly unable to decide between blond and brown, and there is something charmingly restless about him, as if he cannot wait to get going somewhere.

When I approach, he also immediately gets up, giving me a quick hug.

"Nice to see you", he says. "Glad you could make it so soon."

"Likewise", I say, offering him a smile. "Nice place."

"I've walked by a couple of times but never been in, so I thought I'd grab the opportunity." He waves a waiter over. "Something sparkling to start with?"

"Could never say no that. It's a weakness I have."

"Then that makes two of us." He winks, reaching for the wine list. "I find I think so much better, that way."

We talk our way through the menu, charcuterie and cheeses and servings of all shapes and sizes appearing and disappearing throughout the evening, while our glasses are diligently being refilled. As expected, he is a corporate lawyer, and I suspect we know equally little about our respective fields of study. When I tell him what I do for a living, he merely nods, which is a far cry better than terrified.

"So what do you do when you're not working on making the world a better place?" John says between pieces of prosciutto. I cannot help but notice his words do not hold the same warmth as Nico's did, but I tell myself that I am being ridiculous. "I've been golfing a lot with the lads this summer and we still keep it up on the weekends. Then we go out for beers and burgers later. Getting all that fresh air brings out a good appetite."

"I like being outdoors too", I say. "I guess that goes for most kids up north, since there's little else to do. The hills and lakes were close, and we were always roaming around there." Fond memories bring a smile to my face, of long summer days running along the remnants of Hadrian's wall; the trees with low branches where Mike taught me how to climb; the sheep's mad dash when we jumped out from our hiding places behind the rocks, breathless with laughter; the evening swims in the lake, still as a mirror and cold as ice, but none of us minding. "We also grew up skiing, my brother and I – my uncle lives in southern France, so we usually went there for winter holidays."

"I'm afraid I am quite lousy at skiing", he interjects, as if I had asked. He chuckles. "I am a bit scared of heights."

Heights? Is he worried he will fall off the mountain? His apologetic look appears to suggest I should find this endearing somehow, and I almost roll my eyes.

"Anyway, that's about it; annoying how work takes up so much of your time." I shrug. "Same as most people, I guess. I see friends, get in the occasional run, watch plenty of football…"

"Why this interest in football? Did you play?"

"Everyone likes football, don't they?" I shoot back, and he smiles.

"Sure, yeah, I suppose. We usually watch on Sundays, with the lads. Or set up pubs at work for the championships, you know." He nods. "The usual, I guess."

"Well, there you go. It brings people together. It's more than just a game. And although I never played myself – or at least never competitively, we all played for fun in school – my brother did, so I kind of grew up watching him from the stands. I learnt a few tricks, all the terminology, but what really appealed to me were the tactics, the sense of control you can have over your opponent if you only find the keys to unlocking them. It fascinated me." I shake my head. "And then I guess I was just stuck. It's something about the atmosphere, the collective emotions, that get to you in a way few other things can. I mean, that's why we love sports, isn't it? Because it allows us to feel things, to openly show our emotions, without anyone judging."

"And because of the guys, I'm sure?" There is a smirk on his face that I do not like, even as an image flashes before my eyes, of brown eyes flecked with green, of slender fingers running along my spine, and I silently vow I will never reveal that part of myself to him.

"That is an old-fashioned preconception, John", I say admonishingly, my voice stern. "Don't put yourself in a box."

"Sorry", he says, and the smirk falls away. "That was stupid. I mean, a lot of men watch women's sports for their looks, so..." He shrugs. "I guess we're in no way better."

"It's okay", I say, feeling gracious. "There are a lot of women like that. But that doesn't mean we are all the same."

"No", he says, "and that's what I like about you."

He raises his glass for a toast, and I am surprised by how good it feels.

We walk down Northumberland Avenue to Victoria Embankment, still in conversation. I pull my coat tighter around me; the evenings are getting chillier, and I am equally unprepared every year. Ahead, the white spikes of Hungerford Bridge shine bright against the darkening sky, lit from above by blue-white lights. Every time the warmth seeps out of the air, it makes me think of home. Not Ipswich, where I never properly felt like I belonged, but our old home, on the cusp of the widespread Yorkshire moors, and the autumn gradually creeping in, turning the leaves sun-fire yellow and bright flaming orange. My mind drifts as John talks about his latest golf excursion, wondering how large a part of me that never truly left. How much of me is still that little girl, so fascinated by nature and so determined to be a scientist, so oblivious to the rest of the world apart from the gravel roads and the racetrack and the local pitch with trees growing through the wooden stands. I have come a long way, but it sometimes still feels like I am figuring things out as I go, especially when it comes to manoeuvring the parts of life that are not rational and scientifically verifiable.

Something across the street catches my eye then, and I draw to a halt.

"And then", John says, "I...

But I am no longer listening. Parked outside The Grand is a wonder of functional engineering, its outline instantly recognisable even in the dusk, waves of chrome shaping the contours of a raging black sea.

"Wow", I breathe, briefly looking left and right as I cross the street at a jog to get a closer look. "I've never actually seen one of these."

"One of these what?" John has followed me, clearly not certain why. "A sports car?"

"It's not just a sports car", I say, crouching in front of it. The polish is immaculate; it is gleaming, despite the darkness. The centre of a black hole, a pure force of nature. "It's a Bugatti Chiron."

"Oh", John says, tonelessly.

"You're not into cars?" I ask, examining the rear, the single fused taillight creating the impression of a spaceship. He shrugs.

"Not really. I guess I don't really see the point."

"So you've never gone really fast, down a countryside road, feeling like you're about to transcend into another dimension?" I turn my head, smiling at him. "Because trust me, that's among the very best things there are."

"Not so useful in the city though", he says. "And why would you want something like this, anyway? It's obscene."

"Obscene?"

"And impractical. It costs a fortune to keep. What if you scratch it? That alone probably costs thousands of pounds."

"So what car would you chose, instead?" I keep my tone casual, but my eyes remain locked on the Bugatti, my fingers reaching out to touch the sleek lines, the low hood. It oozes speed, recklessness, like a wild animal. Your choice of car says a lot about a person. I think of Brandon in sales, his ostentatious BMW with its oversized grille. I think of Lucy in administration, her harmless house mouse of an Opel. I think of Mike, his sleek Cayman GTS, his pride and joy despite the mortgage gnawing at his pockets.

"A Volvo, perhaps. A Volkswagen." He shrugs. "Sturdy, practical, good value for money."

"You could afford better, though", I say, still circling the car, shamelessly peering inside. "You are not exactly poor, with that job of yours."

"That much money for a car is insane", he scoffs, gesturing. "I wouldn't do it even if I could afford it."

Well, that's where we differ, I think to myself. I do not even know where this innate taste for luxury comes from; it is not that I necessarily *want* things to be expensive, and I do see his point, and yet… Some part of me realises that this is probably where I should appreciate him for his pragmatism, his sound judgement, his family-friendly approach. Like a normal, sensible woman would. *So why don't I?*

"So how about you?" John asks, apparently attempting to draw my attention. I do not even glance up.

"The 1984 Ferrari Testarossa", I say, without blinking. "Pininfarina design, V12 engine, just about clocks 300 km/h at top speed. Fold-up headlights. The gills on the doors are a classic."

For a moment I think his eyes are about to exit their sockets.

"What? Is it so strange that a girl likes cars?" I do not know why I feel the need to challenge him, but I do. Ever since that day when I was five and Dad brought Mike and me to Goodwood, I have had the urge to know what it feels like to sit behind the wheel, to feel that power between your hands, to hear the engine sing beneath your feet. I watch him as he battles with his unease, apparently debating whether it is worth voicing his opinion for fear of the consequences.

"I guess not", he finally says, holding out his arm towards me in a clear *let's go* gesture. I allow him to put his arm around my shoulders as we walk away in the night, but I do not hug him back.

He insists on walking me home, and I let him. It is a pleasant change, having someone to talk to as we trod the familiar streets following the bend of the river. On top of that, John has plenty of things to say, and we cover everything from local politics to attending university in the city to the perks and pains of work travel. He tells me about his younger sister, who wants to be an artist, or a singer, or both.

"She's great", he says, "and very talented. You do wonder how we could possibly have the same genes. But she is quite naïve, and wears her emotions on her sleeve. I'm just afraid she will get hurt." I can hear the fondness and caring in his voice, and lay my hand on his arm in sympathy.

"She's lucky, then, to have a big brother who cares for her", I say. "If you ask me, I don't know where I would be without mine."

When we arrive at my doorstep, it is as though no time at all has elapsed, and now that he has walked all this way, it feels rude and ungrateful to not invite him in.

"Sorry about the mess", I apologise as I throw a stack of towels, residing in plain sight in the middle of the sofa, to the side. "Have been really busy at work." I cringe inwardly at my own words. "Want some coffee?"

"Sure." He sits down on the sofa, one arm leisurely thrown over the headrest. He looks around the flat, no doubt assessing the lack of interior décor and potted plants. I glance over at my sturdy cactus, a true survivor through weeks without proper nourishment as I travel across the country and beyond. It must look empty to an outsider, hardly lived in.

"I travel a lot for work", I feel myself obliged to explain as I put the coffee cups down. "Hence the sparsity of floral arrangements." I wave my hand around vaguely.

"It's fine", he says. "My flat isn't all that either, to be honest. I don't even have a dishwasher, which at this stage of the century is probably positively archaic."

"Gosh, no, that I could never do without. The coffee cups would start a rebellion."

I sit down next to him, sipping my coffee, relishing the warmth and the strong bitter taste. For a moment, there is silence, which, I reflect, might be a first this evening. We have been so absorbed in conversation that its absence now feels like it has its own space in the room, struggling to fill the void.

He takes me by surprise when he reaches for me, his tongue already in my mouth without bothering to start slowly. I go with it, but feel disconnected, as if my body and my mind operate in separate realities.

I want to object, say it is too early, that we should get to know each other properly, but the recollection of my recent exploits makes the words fall off my tongue, unused, and I feel like a hypocrite.

When clothes start to come off, I allow myself to go through the motions, but it feels forced. I do not know where to put my hands, most of all because there is no obvious place where I *want* to put them. John, on the other hand, seems more eager.

"Ouch", I say before I can stop myself. "Take it easy, okay?"

I try to sound casual, but in fact it is not comfortable at all. He does not seem to understand, though, or notice. I squirm, trying to adjust, trying to shift his weight. I bite down on a snide comment about how it probably has been some time since he last visited the gym. From memory, my eyes conjure up an image of a smooth chest with toned muscles, visible as they move beneath the skin, and I decide things might be better off if I shut them altogether.

"Like this, maybe?" I offer, even though I do not feel he deserves it. I try to guide his hand, but there is nothing smooth about his touch, nothing teasing or exciting. It is as if he is doing it, mechanically, without knowing why. Nothing happens, and all I feel is frustration.

Afterwards, alone, I busy myself with the discarded towels. I feel distracted, numb, disappointed, even though I know it is seldom great the first time, before you have had the chance to understand each other. And yet...

Part of me wants to cry. Part of me tells myself this is silly. I have been privileged enough to have tasted perfection. I cannot expect it to be like that, always, or ever. John is a nice guy. He cares. It will get better.

Yet it gnaws at me, however much I try to push it from my mind. Like that line from *Pretty Woman*: *You changed things, and you can't change them back. I want more.*

The question is 'how much more', I ask myself in my head, even as the response is already on my tongue.

I want the fairy-tale.

Chapter 11

By Wednesday lunch I am on my fourth back-to-back meeting, my sixth cup of coffee, and the very edge of my patience, proving that a job can be both inspirational, exciting – and an absolute shitshow. A dull ache is settling in my skull, the insistent throbbing increasing by the minute. I lean back in my chair as the finance representative drones on about budget constraints and changes in allocation per department compared to last year. While I must ensure our activities match up with our finances, the actual mechanics of how the budget is decided and the system in which it is detailed are far beyond both my understanding and my interest. Moreover, this has been going on for more than half an hour after its per calendar invite-designated end, and I already have a backlog of other issues from the previous meetings building up that I need to attend to.

"Bloody hell", I complain to my colleague in commercial, Jasmine, flopping down in a chair by one of the tables in the lunchroom. "This is driving me crazy. They've had this information for *months*, and only now do they think of noticing we don't have enough money to sponsor the symposium? Now, three days before deadline?"

"Tell me about it", she groans, rolling her eyes, the whites contrasting starkly against her dark skin. "I've been busting my ass for weeks getting all that material approved and printed, not to mention express delivery which must have cost a fortune." She shakes her head as she starts chopping vegetables for her salad. I wince; having lunch with Jasmine always makes me feel bad about my I-just-grabbed-whatever-I-found-in-the-freezer leftovers and on-the-go sandwiches. I munch on my chicken panini, trying not to meet her eye.

"How is Dr Stevens' lecture coming along?" she asks, neatly arranging lettuce leaves on a plate. "I assume that's still on, even though the symposium looks as it might not be?"

"We *need* it to be on", I say between bites, trying to look somewhat dignified despite the mustard dressing escaping through my fingers. "He's enthusiastic about it and we have ensured great coverage – remember to thank Carol down at the studio for me again, she's done an amazing job with getting the broadcast up and running – and we'll have a full auditorium as well as several hospitals across the country connecting live via Teams. We still do not, however, have a finalised contract." I breathe heavily through my nostrils as I take another bite. Perhaps it is influenced by my foul mood, but suddenly the chicken tastes unbearably stale, the tomatoes soggy. Despite my stomach's insistent protests, I dump the rest of the sandwich into the bin. Jasmine raises an eyebrow, her fork skewering a perfectly sliced piece of cucumber along with mozzarella and tomatoes.

"How…" But she does not get any further before Sonia appears out of thin air, unceremoniously dropping a pile of papers on the table in front of me out of a perfectly manicured hand.

"Here are the payment details for Dr Stevens", she says. "For the contract." She is gone again before I have time to react, her heels clicking against the floor, her impeccably styled, glossy dark hair swaying behind her as she walks.

"God, she's such a bitch." Jasmine makes a face. "I swear she spends more time on her nails than anything within the walls of this office."

"She just seems to have it in for me, I have no idea why." I shrug. "I might be a bit straight to the point sometimes, but it's not as if she should be expecting me to throw rose petals at her feet for the performance she's presented so far." Rather the opposite, in fact. I make a mental note to talk to my boss about her. If she will not listen to me, perhaps he can make the circumstances of her employment clear. "Anyway, that's the *how* you were looking for. She's the one who's supposed to set up the contracts, but she keeps asking me for information and details in the text, to the point where I wonder whether I just ought to do it all myself to spare me the trouble." I reach for the papers, realising with a sinking feeling that these are not finalised, either. I call after her:

"Sonia? Would you mind coming back for a minute?"

She comes to a reluctant stop in the corridor, deliberately slow in turning around to face me.

"Yes?"

"We need this to be finished *and* signed by tomorrow, before 10 am." I struggle to control my frustration. "I have provided you with everything you need, the only thing remaining is to enter these details into the pre-made form, and then have it signed by Dr Stevens and the Medical Director."

"I thought it was up to you to send it to him for his signature?" She all but rolls her eyes at me, and anger flares up inside me. "This really doesn't feel particularly organised, you know."

"Unfortunately, that is the system we have and must adhere to. The system you, and only you, have access to, which is why I need you to do this for me."

"Don't blame me just because..."

"Would it hurt you to be nice to other people, just once?" I blurt. "And not constantly complain? We're a team here, and we need to help each other." I feel Jasmine's eyes on me without turning, her silent approval.

"Easy for you to say, who get to travel to luxury resorts at the company's expense, while the rest of us do the dirty work. Easy enough to be nice and not to complain then, I wager." I look up at the venom in her voice, her narrowed eyes. More people are arriving in the lunchroom now, and I am unwilling to cause a scene, even though these are things that need to be said, and they clearly need to be said now. “Not exactly like we are equal, now, is it?”

“You do realise it was not a spa retreat, but a business-critical meeting”, I say, my voice even. “And, besides that, unlike some, I actually do my job.”

The ensuing silence is so thick it could be cut with a knife. I realise the stupidity of it, but I cannot for the life of me make myself take it back. Sonia has been nothing but lazy and spiteful since she arrived, and I will not tolerate this from her.

“This is really inappropriate, Sienna”, Alice from regulatory finally says, admonishingly, and out of the corner of my eye, I notice the heads around her nodding in agreement. Internally, I am fuming, cursing them all. Jasmine, on the other hand, looks on the verge of laughter, disappearing into her salad in an unsubtle attempt at disguising it.

“I'm sorry”, I say, eventually, taking a deep breath. “That was uncalled for.” *Not really, but what else can I say?* “Just get the contract ready so we can all have some respite from this whole thing.”

I sense Sonia's dark eyes boring into me long after I have turned my back on her, refusing to let her provoke me into saying things I might regret.

When I leave the office, John is there, just outside as I push open the heavy brass-rimmed door. Surprise shoots through me, but I disguise it with a smile as I walk towards him.

“This is unexpected”, I greet him, and he gives me a light kiss on the cheek. I honestly was not sure I would ever see him again.

“I thought we could go for dinner”, he says. “Got wind of a lovely new place up Marylebone. Seafood, bottle of wine...?”

“That sounds nice”, I agree. “I've had a horrible day at work, so I could do with getting my mind off things.”

We walk down the street towards the tube, him using his briefcase as a battering ram to make space in the throng of people moving towards the platform. This is the worst time of the day to be down here, the moisture and sheer number of bodies thickening the air and increasing the sense of claustrophobia. It is not until we step outside in the calmer area of upper Bond Street that I can breathe freely, and I sigh deeply as I let John in on today's events. It feels good, sharing, and there is obvious sympathy in his voice when he proclaims:

"That's completely out of line. And it shouldn't even be you dealing with it. What does your manager say?"

"I haven't told him yet, but I intend to." I rub my temples in annoyance. "At first, I just thought she was insecure because she was new, and that the snappiness was some kind of defence mechanism, but she's been with us for five months now. This is too much."

"Do you have a good relationship with your manager?" he asks as he holds the door to the restaurant open for me. Square wooden tables line the small, oblique-shaped area, the bar taking centre stage in the middle of the room, pink cushioned bar chairs contrasting against white tiles. Glasses of all shapes and sizes hang upside down above the bar, clinking homely in the gust of wind drifting in through the open door.

"I do", I say, thinking back on how he was willing to bet on me when I arrived fresh from my graduation, with no prior knowledge of the industry but eager to learn and willing to work hard. "He often asks for my judgement when it comes to scientific matters, so I hope he will do it when it comes to employee matters too."

"That's good", he says, signalling for the waiter to bring over a bottle of water and the menu. "I've had every kind of boss – the meek, indecisive ones, the oppressive tyrants, the mental and physical absentees. You learn how to manage them, but ideally you find one whom you enjoy working for, and who appreciates and listens to you. And who has your back, when you need them to."

"He does", I say. "At least I get that impression." I smile at him, feeling myself relax. "Thanks, by the way. I really needed this."

We toast over the small table, before proceeding to order just about everything on the menu. My stomach groans in remembrance of the sandwich I chucked away in disgust, and I realise I am famished. The seafood is to die for, fresh oysters and lobster brought out straight from behind stylish glass counters heaped in ice. I let myself forget everything else and as the evening draws to a close, I find I am thoroughly enjoying myself, something that this morning felt impossible.

"Thanks for tonight", I say as we step outside, the night descending around us. "I had a lovely time."

"Shall I walk you?" There is an expectant note to his voice, a hopefulness that makes me hesitate.

"Last time… Maybe we shouldn't rush this."

"What do you mean? It was good."

No, it wasn't, I think to myself. *And you not even realising is worse.*

"It was a bit early", I opt for. "Perhaps we can take this a bit slower."

"Why? I like you and we're having a good time." He suddenly looks uncertain. "Aren't we?" I wonder again whether I ought to feel sorry for him, and whether I am a bad person for not doing so.

"Because I'm asking you to", I cut him off. "Tonight is not the night, and I need you to respect that, the way you respect my other opinions." I let out a breath. "It doesn't mean I don't like you. I do. It's just been a heck of a day, and I'm going to go home and crash. Alright?"

"Alright." He gives me a kiss on the cheek. "Sweet dreams, and I'll see you soon."

I might be drained, but as my phone reminds me as I step over the threshold, it is Wednesday, which means Champions League group stages. Milan are playing a team from Hungary that I have never heard of, and to be entirely fair, they are neither particularly good, nor is the match particularly interesting. Nevertheless, once

I have started watching I cannot turn the TV off – it seems rude, almost like leaving a lecture mid-speech. I slouch in the sofa, following the proceedings with half my brain on autopilot.

Then, in the sixty-ninth minute, a Milan player is fouled rather violently just outside the box, and the instant commotion draws my attention. The player is still on the ground, grasping his forehead in pain. On the replay, it looks as though he had a nasty encounter with a Hungarian elbow, and said player is now involved in a heated argument with several of the Milanese. I spot Nico, crouching to lay his hand on his teammate's head, speaking to him, and the tender gesture makes something flip over inside me, however hard I try to ignore it. The man on the ground moves his head, slowly, clearly still shaken, or dizzy. I look at the number on his shorts and realise it must be Federico Rossi, the guy whom I saw with Nico at Monza. Clearly, he is a friend as well as a teammate. Nico gets up, anger blatant on his face, and advances on the culprit. Before I have time to blink, he has shoved him, forcefully, in the chest. I can tell they are both yelling, even though I have no way of comprehending the words. Several of Nico's teammates are struggling to hold him back, but the Hungarian player is no better, goading him to keep going, proceeding to spit on the ground before him, and I sense they are mere seconds from throwing hands.

Then I see the referee moving towards the pair of them, determination in his stride. He reaches for his breast pocket, and…

Oh shit, it's going to be a red for that, isn't it?

And it is. For them both. I watch as they go through the motions of loud, elaborate complaints – arms flailing, culturally distinguished hand gestures, most likely borderline offensive phrases. Everyone and their mother know there is not, has never been, any single use in appealing to a referee's empathy, and yet here they all are. But that is not what amazes me most, as I watch Nico walk off the field, shaking his head, whipping his shirt off in anger as he does. My breath hitches for a moment, but his lack of shirt is not the real reason. *At least not the sole reason.* Because I realise that, in some strange way, I found their almost-fight… exciting. Stirring, even.

Since when am I attracted to angry men prone to violence? Rational, practical, sensible me? I squirm at the thought as I watch the players resume their positions, some of them still arguing, visibly agitated, amongst themselves. Rossi is on his feet again, being ushered towards the sidelines by a medic.

Who are you? I scold myself. *And why do you care what he does? He clearly didn't care enough about you.*

It is not until later, in one of those rare moments of perfect clarity just before sleep, that I recognise that it is not so much the wrath itself, but the emotion. The ferocity, the euphoria, the raw passion. It is something else than the strained diplomacy I am faced with at work, the contained frustration, the politely inhibited intimacy.

That's why we love sports, isn't it? I hear myself say in my head. *Because it allows us to feel things. Because it allows us to openly show our emotions, without anyone judging.*

Chapter 12

The next morning, there is an aggressive sound from the doorbell, far earlier than I would ever have set any alarm. I groan in disbelief, forcing myself into a bathrobe and out in the hallway.

"Yes?" My voice is hoarse; I must sound like an old witch, the kind that lives in a cave and only comes out to bring down curses over villagers who have wronged her.

"Flower delivery", the far-too-cheery chap says, pulling at his cap as he does. *God, don't people ever sleep?* "Seems you've got quite the secret admirer." He unloads a huge package in my unprepared arms, wobbling a little as he does, and I nearly drop everything. There is a pot within the package, and a long, gangly stick in the middle of the contraption. *What on Earth?*

"Indeed", I mutter, ripping open the envelope that is flailing like a flag from the bottom of the pot. **Beautiful flowers for a beautiful girl**, I read. **J x.**

"Thank you", I manage to the delivery guy. I hope I have succeeded in keeping a straight face. I never get flowers, and I have no idea how one is expected to react.

"You're welcome." He keeps grinning from ear to ear; perhaps this is his only mood. "Have a nice day."

I close the door behind him and bring the package into the kitchen, unwrapping the white uncontrollable sheet of frail paper as I go. A pristine pot in pale pink emerges, followed by...

Orchids. I frown. He cannot possibly know I hate orchids, never mind how bad I am at taking care of them, and I suppose I have to appreciate the thought. I look around, contemplating how to get rid of them. Just leaving them to their own misery in my apartment somehow feels too cruel; a slow, soul-leeching starvation.

What is wrong with you? I scold myself. *A guy sends flowers, and you immediately want to throw them away?*

I grimace. Maybe they are not so bad after all. Maybe they will not require that much of an effort. Maybe…

In the end, I put them in the window furthest away from the kitchen, where there is at least a glimmer of a chance of sunlight at this time of year. No idea if that will do the trick, but it is survival of the fittest, after all, and I will not be seen mollycoddling a plant, no matter where it came from.

To compensate for my demonic behaviour, I pull out my phone. **Thanks for the flowers**, I write. **They're lovely. Busy this weekend?**

There you go, Rachel, I think, smiling to myself in a sense of triumph. *I am working on it. I am trying.*

We fall into a routine, John and I, almost without intending to, it seems. We meet up after work, go out to eat, share a bottle of wine. We talk about everything and nothing, and sometimes he walks with me, invoking references to old-fashioned aristocratic courtship. By the time November rolls around and it is time for Rachel's and mine annual spa escape, we have not actually spoken about being together, but it is clear we both assume we kind of are. I enjoy the informality of it, at the same time as I cannot help feeling that I am still not quite sure what I am doing.

"Why don't you bring him along?" Rachel asks one evening as we plan the final details of the trip together. "Tom will be sitting at home all on his own and would do well to get out of the house and see some decent male company."

"He spends essentially every minute of his life with you. Don't you think he can manage a few days on his own?" Tom is a great guy, but sometimes I wonder if he is her husband or her puppy.

"Not the whole time, obviously. God, can you imagine men at spa?" She laughs, her newly dyed hair moving in soft tendrils across her shoulders as she does. "I was thinking they could join us for dinner the last night, and then we all go home together."

"All the way to Cotswolds, for dinner? With two people he's never met? Talk about setting a trap."

"I just want to meet him, finally." She pouts, a look of mock dismay she knows I see straight through but may still be softened by.

"Rachel, it's a girls' trip. It's *our* weekend. Do you really want to spoil it by bringing all that testosterone in?" She snorts.

"To be honest, I'm not sure it's *that* much, from your sparse descriptions." I bite down on a grin. *She's not wrong.* "I just thought it might be a good time. He won't be made to feel at a disadvantage coming into our home, and neither will he be forced to host two strangers at his house. This is possibly the least weird situation we could come up with." I roll my eyes, refraining from trying to explain how I am not certain I want to introduce him to anyone at all. Absently, my fingers busy themselves with adjusting the straps on my swimsuit. Rachel does have a point, and I wonder why I keep putting off the inevitable. Perhaps it is better to just get it over with.

Is this really how you ought to feel when you're about to introduce your boyfriend to your best friend?

"I just hope I'm not jinxing anything." I let out a breath. "You know what happened all the other times I introduced you to someone." Rachel tilts her head to one side, looking sympathetic.

"Si…" She shakes her head, at a loss for words, reaching out to hug me instead. I smell the bergamot and white floral notes of her perfume, sense the silent comfort of her sisterhood that will last beyond whatever new ordeal life throws at us. For a moment, the emotional impact of her loyalty overwhelms me. I sniff, blinking back tears, giving her one final squeeze before letting go.

"Fine. I'll talk to him. Just because it's you."

Before leaving for the weekend, I knock on my boss' door. The corner office, as if by the book. Wide windows, curtains drawn aside to reveal magnificent vistas of the city. The top of the pyramid, the epitome of success.

"David, can I talk to you for a minute?"

My boss looks up, impeccable as always in his light blue pressed shirt and camel suit. I sometimes find myself wondering what his wardrobe looks like, whether there are rows upon rows of identical outfits, or whether he has a housekeeper ironing them for him every night.

"Oh, hi, Sienna, good to see you. Almost weekend, at long last. Everything ready for the lecture next week?"

I close my eyes for an instant, grateful that everything finally – *finally* – has come together and we are set to host Dr Stevens in front of three hundred doctors, on site and virtually, on Tuesday.

"Yes", I say, "it is. Actually, though, there is something in relation to this I wanted to talk to you about."

He leans forward over the table, clasping his hands together. His fountain pen balances in its stand next to his elbow, the modern-day rapier of a duellist.

"I am all ears."

"You know Sonia Patel?" I swallow. I do not really know how best to phrase this. I recall the conversation with Rachel about Sophie and the rich client, and my insecurity grows. I have never had to do this before, and once here, I begin to regret it. This is not my job, and I want no part of this. But it is too late now.

"The new Medical Affairs administrator? Sure, what about her?"

"I…" I falter, searching for the right words. It feels mean, but given what I have seen thus far, I cannot perceive any other solution. "There is no nice way to say this, unfortunately, but as I know her trial period will be at its end soon…" I take a deep breath. *Here goes.* "I don't think this is the right place for her."

He raises an eyebrow. Mild interest, without judgement. An encouragement I fail to take to heart. David Lewis is nothing if not fair, but I know he can be cold as a dagger when he needs to be. After all, it is what has taken him this far.

"She has been perfectly civil with me." A brief pause, during which I can feel my pulse picking up speed, my heartbeat bordering on erratic. "Can you elaborate on that?" he asks, and with a growing sense of unease, I do, running through the events – and non-events – of the last months, silently wishing, as I see his eyes narrowing, that I could make it all undone.

Chapter 13

Against all odds, given the frustration and organisational mayhem that has preceded it, Dr Stevens' lecture is a roaring success. As a room full of attendees from the city's most prominent universities and hospitals rise for a spontaneous standing ovation, I shoot Jasmine a glance, silently saluting her immense effort in framing the event. The stage is subtly lit in the company's colours – not so much as to be obtrusive, yet conspicuous enough a detail to be remembered. The entire theme of the décor is designed with faded backdrops of stylised molecular structures, such as mRNA, proteins, or toxins – the key immunogenic components in vaccines. She has been thorough in including them all, so that no one will be able to claim we are partial to one methodology or another; after all, this lecture does not concern our products per se, but rather the evolution and future of the field of vaccinology. I join the applause as I take the stage, saluting our star speaker as well as the engaged and attentive crowd as I proceed to moderate the Q&A session. This is the easy part – I warm them up with a few questions prepared beforehand, and once they get into the flow, more queries from the crowd follow suit. In the end, we almost have to rush through the last comments in order to meet the designated end time, and when I thank them all for coming, it is with a huge, genuine smile on my face.

"That was amazing", I say as I shake Dr Stevens' hand as the crowd begins to mill out of the room. Our headsets are off, and my voice seems strangely small after the echo of the huge conference room. "Again, thank you so much for your time and commitment to this."

"You are most welcome, Sienna", he says, smiling as he collects his computer and charger back into his briefcase. "I enjoyed it very much, and it's always nice when you sense the feeling is mutual within the audience. I daresay we managed to convert some people in here tonight." He winks at me. "Now, what do you say to a toast to success? I for one could do with a cold beer in my speaker-sore throat."

"Most definitely", I say, pulling on my coat. "Why don't you go ahead, and I'll meet you outside? I just need to check a few things off with my colleague."

I find her standing beneath the control panel for the lighting and sound system at the back of the room, instructing two men in grey overalls where to deliver the roll-up boards and infographics that are to be returned to the office.

"Are you ready? We're heading out to grab the customary drink."

"Unfortunately, I won't be able to join you this time." Jasmine looks apologetic. "I have to go straight home; Fred has caught some kind of ear infection and naturally Brian is nervous about handling it himself." She rolls her eyes as she wiggles into her oversized coat, covering her entire outfit completely. Even her fitted upscale dress, stylish yet professional in pale blue, matches the interior this evening.

"No worries", I say, waving goodbye to some of the guests as they saunter by, chatting amongst themselves. This has all run so smoothly, relief washes over me in waves. I feel so light I might soar off the ground any minute. "I'm not ready to go to sleep just yet." She grabs my arm.

"Are you sure it's alright? I feel bad for leaving you alone to do the duties." She nods discreetly towards our guest of honour, waiting at the door.

"Trust me, it'll be fine. This is usually the nice part." I give her a quick hug. "Amazing job today. Truly. The set was stunning – it would never have been the same atmosphere without it." She looks pleased as I wave her off, "Go on now, go take care of your child. And especially your husband." She grins as she pulls her hood up and slips out into the night.

"Shall we?" Dr Stevens says as I catch up with him at the door, which he holds open for me as I nod, and we step out into the chilly London evening. No one is keen to walk far in this temperature, so we sneak in at the first good opportunity to present itself, which happens to be Boyd's, the lobby bar at The Grand. I cannot help but look around as we walk up the steps, but there is no sign of the Bugatti this time, nor any other form of transportation in that league. We sit down at the first available seats, by the edge of the bar, and I clink my glass to his.

"Many thanks again, Dr Stevens", I say. "Tonight was a real success and I for one truly enjoyed listening to you."

"Please, do call me Richard." In his early sixties, Dr Stevens is an elegant man, his once-dark hair streaked with silver grey in a way that appears fashionably interesting rather than dull. As long as I have known him, he has always dressed exquisitely, in navy or charcoal suits, with a tie, one he is now adjusting as he presumably considers his work done for the day.

"You should know it's a pleasure to work with you", he continues. "And I mean that in a distinctly non-creepy way. You're always informed, well-organised, accommodating." He takes a sip of his beer. "The company are lucky to have you. I hope they realise it."

"I hope so too", I say, feeling myself swell a little with pride. Sometimes I tend to forget how good it feels to have someone appreciate the things you do, and why I like my job so much.

"You never considered a career in science?"

"I like to think that's what I have." I offer him a wry smile. "I did enjoy my time doing hands-on research, and that's of course what eventually brought me here, but... Not everyone can be a professor." I shrug. "To be honest, I think I'm a bit too restless, too eager to see change, to drive things forward."

"Definitely not a bad trait to have."

"No", I agree, "but difficult in academia, where everything moves at a snail's pace."

"And how about the corporate intrigues? The organisational constipation? The regulatory shackles? Because in a large enough company, these are all inevitable, in the long run."

"I..." I cannot tell him I find the salary in academia unacceptable and the employment conditions remnants from the stone age. Neither can I say that this was always the idea, the goal I was aiming for, because somehow, in my head, it does not ring as true as I would like it to. "I guess no job is perfect. But I believe I am in a better position to contribute to science, and society, where I am now, rather than where I was."

"I read your thesis, you know."

I flinch. No one ever reads your thesis, except your examination board, who are all but forced to. Even your friends only flip through the acknowledgements to see whether their names made it into print along with some witty remark.

"Your concluding remarks, the discussion on broad-spectrum vaccines for common pandemic viruses, on strategies for capturing not just single strains but the viral core, was compelling. I was seriously impressed." He offers me a pointed look. "But most of all, it showed your passion as a scientist. Your drive, in reaching people, in making a difference."

Shit, he actually did read it. I have no idea what to make of that, whether to be flattered or freaked out.

"I haven't told you about this yet", he says, leaning forward on his elbow, a conspiratorial glint in his eye, "but the truth is I have a side business that is beginning to look quite promising. An old friend of mine from medical school is developing a vaccine against RS viruses, which thus far appears to protect against both the A and B variants, and I have become involved on the managerial end."

"Wow", I say, taken aback he would share this with me. "That could be huge, if it makes it through the trials." My brain runs through the possible socioeconomic implications, the potential decrease in severe childhood disease, the subsequent reduction in sick leave, the respite for public healthcare with less impact among elderly… Not to mention the chance of improving childhood mortality rates due to RSV in low-income countries. *It could be huge indeed.*

"It could", he agrees. "And, if I may, the trials are looking good. We expect finalisation of Phase II any day now, and aim to present the data come spring. As you so eloquently put it, this is undeniably moving rather akin to a snail, but we have high hopes for initiating Phase III already next year."

"Wow", I repeat, feeling somewhat embarrassed that I have not heard of this before. *It's my job to keep up to date on competitors*, I scold myself. *You can't afford to slip up on these things.* "It sounds really exciting."

"If it were successful, would you be interested in joining us? As Medical Lead for the project? Taking us through Phase III and launching the product on the market?"

Medical Lead? Suddenly the bar stool beneath me seems to evaporate, and I have the distinct sensation of falling. My head is spinning. *He wants* me *to head up his Medical organisation?* I realise my hand is gripping at the bar for support.

"I…" I honestly do not know what to say. The mere idea is staggering, both in terms of the business side, if successful, the science behind it, and the role itself. *I don't have enough experience for this. Why does he want me?* People do not just get handpicked into managerial positions within just a few years after graduation.

He knocks back the last of his beer and, standing, extends his hand. I shake it, grateful for the firm, grounded grip, and he smiles at me.

"Think about it. I fully understand it's a risky move, stepping over to a start-up when you're already in a well-established, solid organisation. But from what I've seen and heard from you", he raises an eyebrow, "I think you would be a perfect fit."

"Thank you", I say, struggling to breathe normally, yet forcing myself to smile back. "I certainly will."

"I'll share the Phase II results with you as soon as they become available", he says in parting, "so that you have a clearer perception of what we're talking about."

It takes several minutes before I manage to stand, all but forgetting to pay the bill. My knuckles are white from holding on to the golden-rimmed counter, and there is a buzz in my ears, as if from standing in the blast of a strong wind. But it is a warm, intriguing buzz – a tropical whirlwind rather than a damning winter hailstorm – and there is a sense of opportunity here that, once the initial shock has abated, thrills me. The ramifications of this are daunting, terrifying even, but nonetheless, exhilarating.

As I step outside, wrapping my scarf around my neck, I catch a movement out of the corner of my eye. A flash of metal in the headlights of a cab, spokes glinting as wheels are quickly gaining speed. A fashionably styled bundle of dark hair, zigzagging between pedestrians on their way to the theatre district, its movement somehow familiar; it is too far away to tell, but I can easily imagine the perfectly manicured nails gripping the handlebars.

Is that Sonia? I crane my neck, trying to get a clearer view of the woman on the bike, but she has already disappeared in the crowd.

On my way home, I buy a *I shouldn't, but I've earned it*-pizza and catch the last twenty minutes of Milan's game. I notice this too has become a habit, more than ever before. I would watch whichever games were on at the time I felt like watching, give or take a certain bias. Now, I find myself keeping track of kick-off times, working my calendar around match day, even though it does – apparently – not always work out. I tell myself it is ridiculous as he has no way of knowing that I am watching, and would not care even if he did. *He left.*

After the final whistle, it is Nico doing the interviews. He seems at ease, smiling as the camera team struggles with the headset and saying something, presumably a pun at the technology, in Italian. He looks… *God, he looks good.* I curse my weak mind, but there is no escaping it. His hair falls charmingly into his eyes, the dark curls even more pronounced when damp with sweat, and as he strokes his chin, I cannot help but see the two-day stubble suits him. He adjusts the earpieces, giving the clearly anxious producer thumbs up.

"*Buona sera*, Nicolo, and thanks for bearing with us. First of all, congratulations on yet another solid victory…"

I absorb the conversation as I work my way through my now long-since cold dinner, taking in his measured responses, his expressive gestures, the tiny crease appearing between his eyebrows as he concentrates on the question, the way his eyes seem to smile as if at a joke only he can understand.

I realise despite my best efforts, I am unable to force myself to dislike him. He might have let me down, but not in the way the others did. He made no promises, gave me no reason to expect anything. And I find myself wishing he would have. It would have been easier, then, to make myself forget. To let go.

"What's your favourite trick?" the reporter asks him, and he chuckles, one hand rubbing his neck as he clearly considers his answer.

"Ah, that's a tough one. Hmm." He bites his lip. "I do like the *sombrero*, when you flip the ball over the head of your opponent", he eventually says, "but what I've always wanted to do in a big game is the *rabona*. You know, where you cross your leading foot behind the other leg and hit the ball…"

"Yes, yes", the reporter nods. "So, can we expect to see one of these in the upcoming games?" He winks. "Or are you saving it for the Euros, maybe?"

"We'll see, we'll see", Nico says, all smiles. "There is still more than half the season left, so this is where our full focus lies right now." He nods and waves his thanks as he takes off down the corridor towards the dressing room. The broadcast keeps rolling as I imagine him dancing his way through the defence, twisting up players left and right, his right foot connecting with the ball behind his left before it sails into the net.

I hope you get to do it, one day, I find myself thinking, knowing full well I should not care as much as I do.

Chapter 14

There are few things I love more than the utter relaxation that comes from being in the water, the sense of absolute freedom, letting the foreign element absorb you entirely in a gentle, soothing embrace.

I lean back, allowing the cool water to soak my scalp, my hair spreading around me like flower petals. Outside, the leaves have turned every shade and colour of yellow, orange, blood-red and chocolate brown, the palette of fall spread across the canopy as if by a painter's brush. The air is frigid, I know from the short walk over from the parking lot, but in here, the steam rises from the hot baths at the far end of the room, enveloping the wooden-rimmed floor-to-ceiling windows in a gentle mist that seems to alter the surrounding landscape. Softening it, removing the roughness around the edges, and instead leaving a welcoming cushion on which to pleasantly fall. In the other room, Rachel is enjoying her second massage session of the day, leaving me temporarily alone in tranquil silence.

This place was old already when we first came here, but it is also part of our history, Rachel's and mine. A constant throughout the years, like that roundabout at your block that you always have to circle whether you are leaving or coming home. Sometimes I wonder whether it also has a memory, whether the joys and sorrows experienced here are ingrained in the walls. Our successes, our failures; wood and glass and stone given a mind and spirit of their own. The elation and physical exhaustion after completing my first half-marathon, Rachel's frustrated attempts at learning how to drive with a manual transmission, the seemingly never-ending hangover after our last exams, the emptiness after…

I dive beneath the surface, shutting my eyes and ears to the unbidden images. Perhaps that is the true reason why I always leave here feeling rejuvenated; the water seemingly shouldering my burdens while I am left, relieved, to the almost reverent stillness.

For how long, though? I am protective of this place, I realise, of its healing power, and the thought of the guys' presence here makes me uneasy. It is an intrusion, their every step on the old wooden floors an act of trespassing into this sanctum of our friendship, and as I get out of the pool and submit myself to the hot spray of the shower, merely prolonging the inevitable, I know I am not ready. For the magic to dissolve, and to shoulder the burdens left behind here on my own.

John and Tom arrive, predictably, right on time for pre-drinks before dinner on Saturday. I wait around the lounge early, wanting to greet them before Rachel launches into interrogation mode. Tom gives me a quick one-armed hug and slips off to surprise his wife, who most likely is still in the shower.

"Good to see you", John says as we hug, and he gives me a quick kiss. "Feel relaxed yet?"

"Very", I confirm, smiling. "This is one of my real happy places. We first came here on a whim while we were still in university, Rachel's mum had some form of gift certificate she couldn't use, and we just loved it. We've been coming back every year since."

"It's lovely", he says, surveying the thick wooden beams that span the high ceiling, the stone walls, returned to their former glory by years of diligent restoration and commitment by the local community. This is a treasure and source of pride, which is noticeable in everything from the familiarity of the staff to the quality of the highly rated restaurant.

“How was your week?” I ask, as an attentive waiter comes to serve us champagne. Rachel and Tom are yet to join us, and I feel on edge, eager to get the awkward introductions over with. I fidget with my watch, sipping the champagne far too quickly.

“Fine”, he says, shrugging. “There was some hassle over a trial report, but we managed to get it sorted just before we left. Otherwise, it’s mostly been planning, actually, setting up the calendar for the coming months.”

“Sounds comfortable enough”, I tease.

“Well, I’ve been thinking. Turns out I have a conference in Paris first week of February”, he says. “Why don’t you come down there and spend the weekend afterwards?”

I keep my face straight. Contrary to popular opinion, I am not convinced about Paris as a romantic city, but I can see he has a point. It is close by and a short enough time not to be a huge commitment, yet a decent opportunity to show whether we can do this together.

“Sounds good”, I say, refraining from voicing my concern about the inevitability of sharing rooms and all that it entails. *Why don’t I think it’s a good idea? Why can’t I be more enthusiastic?* “Let’s talk about it when we’re back in London and look into details?”

“There he is! Ah, finally!” Rachel all but rushes at John, beaming from ear to ear as she forgoes his outstretched hand and immediately throws her arms around him. “It’s so good to finally meet you! I’ve only heard dreadful things, of course.”

Mortified, I roll my eyes, but John only laughs and bends to give her a polite kiss on the cheek instead, quipping “If anything I’ve heard from Sienna is true, I gather the pleasure is all mine. Nice of you to have me. Tom did tell me on the train he hasn’t been allowed in here before either, so I consider this an honour.”

“That’s what he told you?” Rachel scoffs. “Believe me, he’s been invited. He was just too intimidated by the sheer extent of overpowering female energy.”

“Well, I hope I am up to the task”, John chuckles. “I’m looking forward to it. I’ve heard the food here is amazing.”

Dinner is set in the old barn, the ceiling reaching high above our heads, raw wood polished smooth and set in irregular patterns against the whitewashed walls, the impression almost that of a simple country church. The tables are solid wood, knotholes and growth rings visible beneath the gloriously elegant tabletop setup, handcrafted ceramic plates and handblown glass surrounded by decorative clinging vines, herbs and moss, all no doubt grown on the premises. In contrast, the dishes are all modern compositions, every course a sight for sore eyes in terms of colour, presentation, and flavour combination, and after the initial pleasantries, conversation is uninhibited, everyone in awe over the attention to detail and the subtle yet intriguing taste sensations that explode in our mouths. The effortless fusion between the rustic and the elegant, farm and fancy, Middle Age and modern, is another thing I love about this place, the way time has both managed to move forward and stand still.

Perhaps it is because I can relate? I reflect, as the others instigate yet another toast. I smile, joining them, yet not quite there. *Because I am, in certain ways, still stuck, even while I’m forced to keep moving?*

“That was nice”, Rachel says as we get into bed, full and happy after six courses with accompanying wines. She winks at me. “John is nice, too.” I groan, hoping it serves as an acknowledgement without the need for further comment.

“He wants me to come with him to Paris.”

“Well, hello? You say it like it’s a question.”

“That means sharing rooms. Beds.” I sound like an idiot and Rachel looks at me accordingly.

“I don’t know what your perception of a relationship entails”, she says slowly, as if manually counting my brain cells, “but that usually counts as standard procedure. You mean you haven’t…”

"We have", I say. "Hence the question."

"Oh." For once, Rachel is at a loss for words, and I am grateful.

"I just don't… feel it." I sigh. "It's hard to explain, but I think you know what I mean? All these guys, they have been nice and all, but…"

Except that once. That one time, that will never come again.

"I do know what you mean." Rachel looks surprisingly serious as I shake my head. Flipping back the duvet, she moves with purpose, crouching in front of the minibar. I raise an eyebrow as she remerges a moment later, placing a piccolo bottle of champagne and a jar of olives on the nightstand between us.

"At this hour? You didn't get enough at dinner, I see?"

"This conversation clearly calls for measures." She looks meaningly at me, and her tone brooks no argument. "Go on."

"I don't know, maybe there is something wrong with me. But I just can't seem to tell whether there is a difference between this and anything else, and something tells me that if there was a manual on these things, that is not what it would say. I would have guessed it would say something along the lines of 'when you know, you know'."

"You deserve to be happy, you know." Rachel pinches an olive between two perfectly manicured fingers, chewing at it as she observes me. "You deserve to feel all these things; it's not some outrageous flight of fancy. People in general, believe it or not, actually feel attracted to their partners." I roll my eyes.

"Yeah, I know. On an objective level, I know. But it's not that simple."

"What isn't?" She leans back, champagne glass in hand.

"Any of it. I don't know, maybe the reason is I'm just not over…"

"Who, Nathan? Sod him, he was useless."

"No", I say, letting out a slow, long exhalation. "Not Nathan."

"*That* was a long time ago, and given you've been seeing multiple guys since then, you better well be over it. You need to *allow* yourself to be. He can't be permitted to take this from you, too."

"Take what?" I frown, not following.

"Darling." Rachel rolls her eyes. "*Really.* You are brilliant and gorgeous and I love you to bits, but are you really going to make me explain this?"

"Explain what?" I sip my wine, at this point with an inkling of what type of speech is coming but regardless playing it as cool as I possibly can.

"You need to *want* the guy", Rachel says, exasperation obvious in her voice. "You can't just go around thinking 'this is fine'. It's not fine. If he's not making you feel like you're on fucking fire from within, I'm sorry love, but then he ain't right for you."

I did feel something like that for Nico, more than I had any right to feel, and clearly, I'm not over that either.

"That simple, huh?" I lean back, eyeing her over the rim of my glass. "You think we all get to choose that way?" I shake my head. "Was that what it felt like when you met Tom? Provided that you can still recall the dawn of time." She smiles.

"No. Not from the beginning. In fact, I thought he was rather dull. Don't get me wrong, he was sweet and funny and all, but I just didn't get all worked up about it. Then gradually we spoke more, and that connection led to another form of intimacy, which eventually became attraction. It came to a point when I couldn't tear my eyes away when he walked into the room, and I found myself wondering what happened." She smiles, adding with a slight shake of her head, "All I'm saying is, it needs to be there, otherwise you're fooling yourself into thinking that this will work. But it can grow into being gradually, too. You just need to give him – and yourself – the chance."

"I suppose."

"He's a good one, Si. He really is."

"Yeah", I say. "He is."

"And stable. Safe. Exactly what you want."

No, I find myself thinking. *It might be what I need, but I'm no longer sure it's what I want.*

Chapter 15

Mike calls me so early on Monday morning, a cold chill grips my heart and I answer with my breath caught in my throat.

"What's going on? Has something happened?"

"I am henceforth willing to humbly accept your eternal gratitude", he says, the pride obvious in his voice, and I let out a sigh.

"God, you're annoying. I thought you were about to tell me Dad had a heart attack or something. You never call this early. Have you even had coffee yet?"

"Do you want to hear this or not?" His attempt at mock irritation fails to mask the excitement beneath, and I smile to myself, curious now.

"Alright, spill."

"I've got us tickets."

"To the Euros?" I punch the air with the hand not holding my phone, startling an older woman passing by on the sidewalk. "That's awesome!"

"Not just the Euros", he says, his smugness apparent through the line of static. "To the final."

I gasp. "No way."

"Way", he laughs, so pleased with himself I have to laugh too. "Six in total, that was the maximum I could buy."

"Mike, wow." I shake my head. "That's going to be incredible. Imagine England making it to the final."

"It'll be mad", he agrees. "Bloody hell, feels like ages since we last went to Wembley. Can't wait."

"You're the best", I say. "I owe you big time."

I smile to myself as I end the call, pushing open the door to the office. This really is the best possible outcome – watching the entire tournament, knowing the ultimate experience is yet to come. Finally, I have something to truly look forward to.

Within a minute of entering the building, Jasmine stops me in the corridor, a peculiar look on her face.

"Did you hear about Sonia?"

"What about her?" I drop my bag on the floor and slip out of my coat.

"She's been let go. You wouldn't have had anything to do with that, would you?" She cocks an eyebrow at me, and despite the relief I should be feeling, something nags uncomfortably at my stomach. The memory of the woman on the bike, outside the bar. The malice in her words, right here, within these walls.

"I have no idea what you mean." I shrug, hoping it will suffice, but her smile only broadens.

"Thank God we're finally rid of her. You should have seen the tantrum she threw. Unbelievable."

"Tantrum?" I do not like the feeling of this, where this is going.

"Oh yes, you would have thought she was five years old. Started screaming at David, throwing stationery around and all. Shoved her desk's entire contents straight into the bin without discrimination so that yours truly had to go through everything and see what needed salvaging." Her shoulders shake with restrained laughter. "It was quite a show, I tell you. But hey", she nudges me, "don't look so grim. It's not like she can blame you, is it?"

Is it? She should blame herself and her behaviour, but as I sink into the chair by my desk, I cannot shake the feeling that I have done something wrong. Deep down, I know had to say something, but now I suddenly feel like the villain, the bitter hag who always must have her way, who is neither patient nor supportive but runs to the boss behind her colleagues' backs.

"Funny thing though", Jasmine muses. "If I remember correctly, David hired her himself. It's not often he makes a complete mistake like that."

Only half listening, I nod, surveying the city skyline through the curtain walls. Out there, the smooth black and silver shimmers of The Gherkin and the stark blue sharpness of The Shard stand out as landmarks of the business district, brightly shining monuments to power, money, and success. Above the crowd, above the clouds; top of the building, top of the world.

Is this not the apex of it all, the pinnacle towards which all hard work is aimed? I think about what Dr Stevens – *Richard* – said about corporate intrigues and realise this is the very thing he was referring to, the in-house drama and reluctance to handle open conflict, leadership disconnected from daily activities, behind closed doors.

When did it become so much paperwork, so many internal meetings, far removed from the client and the patient? For how long has more of my time been devoted to administrative duties, contract procedures, and regulatory approvals than to science? I think back on the RS virus initiative that has seemingly passed us all by. Brought in here, that information would wreak more havoc than the detonation of a landmine, the ensuing panic as certain as after a gunshot in a poultry house. Is this what success really is: constantly looking over your shoulder, suspicious of everyone who might dare to climb the tower and sink their teeth in your back? It is similar to sitting back with eleven men in the box and waiting for your opponent to make a fatal, last-minute mistake that allows you to score on the counterattack. Should we not do more than merely react? Should we not aim to be imaginative, innovative, inspiring? Was that not the purpose with which the company was once founded?

We should be more than this, I think. *Better.*

But I wonder how much someone like me is able to change, and how far I am prepared to go to make it happen.

That night, I dream again. This time, though, it is far more realistic, almost like a recording, a sepia tinge to the old footage. Fleeting images, as if viewed through a window in motion, of medieval stone towers, walled towns and picturesque cottages lining lawns and meadows.

A lake, flanked by age-old oak trees, a faint rustle among their knobbly branches, a whisper from a bygone era.

A ruin, the old monastery reduced to rock piles and long-lost memories, the almost indiscernible echo from the footsteps of nameless shadows.

I know what comes next: the crossroads at the village border, the wooden sign visible from afar, as distinctive and unremitting as the symbol it emulates. I know the houses that lie beyond, know the names and faces of the people who live there.

I am running up the hill, grass lush and green beneath my bare feet, but I am not drawing nearer, and the faster I run, the more it feels as if I am going backwards.

Chapter 16

Under the ruse of investigating competitive intelligence, I work from home as the week draws to a close. Usually, I prefer to see my colleagues, follow the banter and the gossip, not to mention using the office as a reprieve from the misery of my soulless apartment, but this time I need the peace and quiet, and most of all the privacy. Going back as far as the publication databases will allow me, I spend hours poring over the comings and goings of Dr Richard Stevens and his associate. At fifty-six, Professor Alistair McKenna is clearly a star, with a PhD from Edinburgh, expedited in only two and a half years, sabbaticals at Stanford and Cambridge, his own research group at Imperial College, and a massive R01 grant from NIH for computational modelling of vaccine protein subunits. Currently onto his third marriage with four children, he seems the type to be riding high and fast, his fingers in all kinds of pies. Perhaps he needs Richard for stability as much as anything else, his firm common sense a counterpart to his own wild creativity? At the same time, he seems perfectly capable of running a business, as the company appears to have grown exponentially over the last few years, attracting interest from both venture capitalists and potential big pharma buyers. Thus far, though, they have managed to stay independent, working mainly out of grant money. Moreover, McKenna appears exceedingly thorough, seemingly handpicking his associates, his group composed of equal numbers of clinicians and molecular scientists, covering all angles from immunogenicity of viral epitopes to long-term safety.

I cannot deny I am impressed. They are clearly onto something big, and I realise the scientist in me is more than intrigued. I want them to succeed, and somehow, I want to be part of it.

I catch John for a quick drink before he heads straight off to what he refers to as his 'Boys & Burgers' golf weekend. He wears a faded pink polo shirt, buttoned all the way up, and I am instantly reminded why I have never quite warmed to golfers' fashion. There are very few people below the age of fifty who successfully pull that look off. *Perhaps it's just a law school thing*, I think to myself, remembering the law students at university, with their men's clubs and whisky tastings, trying to look as if they were already old men, wise from the court rooms of the world.

"I know you're off to play golf now, but just so you know, you'll be watching football this summer", I say, unable to contain my excitement as I tell him about Mike's coup with the tickets. "It'll be you and me, Mike, Rachel and Tom, and I suppose a friend of Mike's, if his fiancée lets him out of the house." I slide into the seat next to him, thankfully accepting the glass of wine he has already ordered for me.

"Sounds great. Speaking of tickets, I've booked everything now", John says, taking a swig of his beer.

"Booked what?" I frown.

"Paris. For the conference, like we talked about. Hotel Le Bellechasse, close to the Musée de Orsay. We get there Wednesday morning and stay until Saturday lunch."

"Hold on." I put up my hand. "First off, we haven't talked about anything. You said the conference was until Friday lunch, and then I would come for the weekend. You don't really expect me to come for less than twenty-four hours, do you?"

"Nah, that would be pretty short, I agree. So why don't you just come Wednesday evening, or Thursday?"

"And do what, be your conference sidekick? Or entertain myself while you're working?" I clench a fist in my lap to prevent the frustration I am feeling from boiling over. “I do work, you know. I can’t just take off in the middle of the week.” Even as I say it, my own hypocritical sense of duty makes me cringe. *Like you didn’t call in sick from Ancona*, a familiar voice in my head taunts. But I insist to myself this is different. *He didn’t even ask.*

“Of course not”, John says. “We’ll spend time, I’ll not be there around the clock. You could do with a few days off.”

“I definitely could”, I respond, fighting to keep my voice in check, “but that is not the point. We *agreed* on something, then you went ahead – without my knowledge – and booked something else. *That’s* the point. Also, I have external meetings that Thursday. Which you would have known, had you bothered to ask.”

He looks at me over the rim of his glass, as if judging whether he should speak or stay silent. *Go on*, I find myself urging him. *Argue back. Show me you have the guts.*

But in the end, he just shakes his head.

“Well, yeah, I probably should have.” He sighs. “I guess we’ll have to do it some other time, then.”

And just like that, despite the fact that I am actually furious with him, my anger deflates. As I walk out, watching him gather his golf clubs and head in the opposite direction, I feel nothing but empty.

Chapter 17

We're collecting money for a gift for Laura's baby, the text comes from Sean. **A boy, she's named him Nicholas.** My insides turn at the name, the universe taunting me, conspiring against me as a constant reminder. **You want in?**

Sure, I type. **Great idea. I'll wire you the money.** And then, in a spur of pure spontaneity, **Hey, you busy this eve? Fancy a beer after work?**

As it is just the two of us, we decide against The Wellington, striving to breach new waters. I do not venture to Southbank often, but when I do it always strikes me how much I enjoy the relaxed, playful vibe, the colourful installations, the almost playground-like bars and pub joints merged in with art galleries, led by the flagship Tate Modern, the reconstructed medieval The Globe theatre, and sleek architectural wonders in geometric shapes of glass and steel. We stroll aimlessly until Sean points beneath a bridge and around the corner, a red double-decker bus is parked up in a small square. The windows are open to reveal a bustling, if somewhat cramped, bar counter, and there is a sign hanging off one of the side mirrors: *The Bloody Oyster.* Crates, barrels and what looks like discarded cinema chairs are arranged in front into a makeshift seating area.

"What is this place?" I ask, unable to hide the marvel in my voice. I have never heard of this before.

"This, my dear, is what we call a quality pop-up. Best Bloody Marys in London. And cracking oysters, at that."

Bewildered, I take a seat – folding out the cinema chair and dusting it off – as Sean brings over a tray of oysters on ice and two large, tomato-red drinks sprouting proud celery sticks. He sets it all down on the upturned wooden box – having once carried coffee beans from Ecuador, judging by the label on the side – and grins at me.

"Amazing", I say, leaning forward to grasp a shell. "I had no idea this existed." I slurp the mollusc down, relishing the fresh taste of saltwater and sea, sprinkled with just the right amount of citrus and Tabasco. "Thanks for taking me."

"Anytime." He grins. "I thought it's time you discovered this town has more to offer than just high-end bars and sloppy pubs."

I stick my tongue out at him, and take a sip of my drink. Something I only ever order at brunches or airplanes, it works surprisingly well in this context. I pull my jacket closer around me; it is a nice evening, the skies for once clear and the temperature pleasant, if not exactly warm. If someone had told me I would be having drinks outdoors in London at this time of year I would have laughed in their face.

We finish our tray and get another one, topping up our drinks as we go. We laugh, reminiscing old memories from the lab, the people who have come and gone, the things that never turned out the way we once thought they would. There is a melancholy behind the laughter, I sense, from both of us, the unforgiving sensation of the long since end of an era we are reluctant to let go, and the times past that will not be repeated, because time itself has moved on. Perhaps that is what prompts the question, as I know I cannot ask about his defence date, but still wish to come away with answers.

"Sean, can I ask you something?"

"Sure." He glances up, his greyish eyes fixed on me. I swallow, uncertain if this is a good idea.

"Why didn't we… ever… I mean…"

To my surprise, his face lights up in a grin.

"Are you referring to the infamous snogging at the Müller-Thompson group's Christmas party?"

Oh God, I thought he had forgotten. At least I have done my very best to act as thought that evening never happened, that scene in particular indefinitely erased from memory.

"I... well... I suppose, yes."

He reaches out to me then, and for a moment I think he will hug me, or even something else, but instead, he gently touches my cheek, adjusting a loose strand of hair behind my ear.

"No, Si", he says, and his voice is unusually low and serious. "Truth is, you're too wild for me."

"Too *wild*?" Of all the things I might have prepared myself to hear, this was not it.

"It's always something happening with you; always new things, constantly moving. The fast cars, the high-fly job, the fancy bars... Don't get me wrong, I think it's great your career is going so well, and I'm happy for you because I like *you* as a person. But at the end of the day, I am a farm boy by birth, and this is all a bit too much for me." He shrugs self-consciously. "Perhaps that's why I haven't finished yet, although, by all means, I should have. Perhaps the academic lull suits me just fine." He smiles, and despite his words a trace of sadness clouds his eyes.

I let out a long breath, steading myself. I did not know what to expect, bringing this up, but I had not anticipated that a rejection I did not even see was in the cards could hurt the way it does.

"So ambition is not attractive, is that what you're saying?" It comes out harsher than I intended, and I bite my lip.

"On the contrary, ambition is very attractive. Don't ever let anyone take that away from you. What I'm saying is that you just need someone who can match your speed."

My speed. I do not know whether to laugh or cry. Is that not exactly the problem? That I have been running all this time, unable to slow down for fear of the emptiness I left behind catching up with me?

"You know", I begin, slowly, my voice suddenly shaky. I never talk about this. "Before I came here… Before grad school. I… I almost didn't start. I was with someone – his name was Martin, and we were at uni together. He always wanted to move out to the country, back where we both came from, and wanted me to follow him. So I almost gave up my position." I take a deep breath, trying not to think of the phone call to my mother where she urged me to follow my heart, because it was the one thing I would not regret. And then… "Guess what happened?"

"He left you?" Sean's voice is brimming with sympathy, a sympathy I for once know I deserve but am not certain I can handle.

"He told my mother he was going to propose. We were way too young, of course, but my mother was so excited, she thought this was absolutely marvellous. He came over for afternoon tea and she invited the whole clan, my aunt and uncle and my cousins, who still live up north. We made all these plans, talked about where we would live, what the house would look like, how he already had work guaranteed in the family firm."

The memories wash over me, unbidden, rushing in over the barricades I have so carefully built, threatening to drown me. The flowery bedsheets, the creaking of the staircase, the faint laughter. The lively conversation downstairs, fading into the background behind the increasingly frenzied beating of my own heart.

"I found him, in my bedroom. With my cousin." I take a deep breath to steady myself, but it is doing very little for the way my hands cannot seem to stop shaking. I dare not look at him. The light falling in through the slanted windows, just so. The Depeche Mode posters on the wall, the framed picture of Mike and I with our dad at Silverstone. The doors to my wardrobe, slightly ajar to reveal the dresses I had outgrown. The remnants of my teenage years, the rosy haze of a youthful dream, and the violation of a shattered promise.

"And he had the nerve to say how much more convenient it would all be when we moved up north, so that our families would be closer to one another."

There. I said it. The silence, stretching into oblivion, a thick blanket pulled down by weights. I realise a shaky, pent-up breath.

"So that's why you don't let people close. Why you always have something to prove." It is not a question, so I cannot be expected to answer.

"That's why I won't let anyone stop me from doing what I want in my career", I reply, my knuckles straining as I dig my nails into the burgundy velvet of the old cinema seat. "Anyone who thinks they have a right to decide what I do or not do with my life, can, respectfully, fuck off."

I refrain from telling him how it tore my insides apart. How it broke my trust for my mother, whom I somehow – and, I fully realise, unfairly – believed ought to have known better, with her years of experience, who should have been more sceptical and less supportive. How it ruined the relationship between her and her sister, who are scarcely on speaking terms after Mike barged in and unceremoniously threatened to throttle both Martin and Evelyn on the spot. The pregnancy announcement must have been the first she has heard from her in years. Was it truly a brag, I now wonder, or an attempt at repair while there is still anything left to salvage?

"But…?" Sean enquires, leaning forward. "Because I do sense a *but* in there."

"They're having a baby now. And even though that's not the thing, that's exactly what I wasn't ready for, it just…"

"…feels unfair, that they just moved right on with their lives, together, while yours was turned completely upside down", Sean fills in. I exhale, my throat thick and sore, a raw wound ripped open.

"It does", I croak, hating my own voice, the weakness in it. "As if somehow, I'm the failure, the one who doesn't have her life sorted, who still doesn't bother to cook for one, who always travels alone. It doesn't seem to matter what else I do."

"I thought you travelled alone for work?" Sean frowns. "That's not the same."

"And I hate it." I down my glass. "If something happens, I know I'll definitely die alone."

"What? That's what you're thinking about? Ugh, that's so depressing. Why haven't you ever told me?"

"Because it's depressing. I'm telling you now, am I not?" I sigh. "It's all supposed to be this 'independent businesswoman' thing, but I can't stand it. It's not that I am not capable or organised enough, or anything like that, it just feels pathetic."

"Si…" Sean gets up this time, and I have to rise to, as he puts his arms around me and pulls me into a firm hug. I close my eyes, pushing the tears back forcefully, so hard my temples hurt. *I will not cry. Not here, not now. I can't, because if I start, I might not be able to stop.*

Then I feel his hand cup the back of my aching skull, and, as if reading my mind, Sean whispers in my ear:

"You know, it's okay to be vulnerable sometimes."

Chapter 18

Sienna, may I borrow you for minute?"

As usual, David Lewis' word is law, and thus he does not wait for an answer. I follow him into his office, slightly bewildered, shutting the door behind me. For good measure, I pull down the blinds for complete discretion. I am not sure why, or what I am expecting, but something about his behaviour feels ominous.

"How are you?" he says, and that alone is unsettling. He might be my boss, and while he is often appreciative of my work, I can count the number of times he has engaged in my emotional well-being on one hand.

"Fine, thanks", I say warily. "What's on your mind?"

"It has come to my attention that there have been some issues regarding verbal conduct, on your part, this past month." I frown.

"Is this about what I said in the lunchroom?" It has been weeks since Sonia was dismissed, and I had thought – hoped – we would be past this by now.

"Not really. Or maybe it has to do with that as well, but the concern is mainly the deeper meaning behind it." He leans forward over his desk, all professionalism in his tailored attire. "Look, there is no good way to put this. It is my duty as your manager to inform you there has been a discrimination charge filed against you."

It feels like someone has ripped the carpet out from beneath my feet.

"Discrimination charge?" I repeat, incredulous. "I beg your pardon?"

"And there will have to be an internal investigation." He sighs. "I'm sorry, Sienna, but unfortunately there is no way around this."

"But she's British!" I blurt. "How in the…"

He looks admonishingly at me.

"I think you know what I mean", he says, slowly. "And I would prefer it if we didn't throw around names, or make assumptions, in order to handle this as discreetly as possible. The company cannot afford to take this lightly, regardless of how groundless the charges may be."

Blatant anger flares through me, and any unease I might have previously felt with regards to Sonia losing her job evaporates in an instant. *How dare she?* I did come here with the aim of success, of making a name for myself outside academia. But certainly not to forget who I am and what matters to me. This is an insult to the fundamental values upon which I have been brought up, a slap in the face of everything I am.

"I will attest to not utilising the most appropriate vocabulary", I say, as professional as I can possibly manage, "but I will emphasise that I stand for everything I have said, because I believe it to be the truth." I place my palms on his desk. The look in his steely grey eyes unnerves me, but I force myself to not look away. "I realise this is probably not the best way to phrase this, but I couldn't care less where she – or anyone in her family, or anyone else for that matter – comes from, as long as she does what she's here to do. Point is, she is lazy and disdainful and acts as if every task you put her to is a personal offence. It's not working and by no means should we keep her employed. That was the point I made, and you chose to listen. And it seems she has not been facing up to this fact particularly well. How is this my problem?"

"What about Dr Stevens?"

"What about him?" I am furious now, and I know myself well enough to be aware of the danger. I am mere seconds from saying something that could send me packing up my desk in an instant.

Presumably something referring to his arrogance, and the body part he is currently far too comfortably perched on.

"I am told you went out together after his lecture. Alone." He raises an eyebrow.

"Jasmine had a sick child at home. What was I supposed to do, stand the man up?"

"Still." He leans back in his chair, tilting slightly as he presses his fingertips together. "All things considered; you went out for a drink. Just the two of you."

Does he enjoy this? I wonder. *Is he testing me, seeing whether I will break or fight back?*

"Sir", I say, making an effort to keep my voice level, "with all due respect, this is out of order, and you know it. It is common practice for us to take our clients to dinner or similar in conjunction with a meeting or a consultancy service. If you are suggesting anything of unsavoury nature occurred, for God knows what reason, I can assure you it did not." *He also offered me a job, but I can't tell you about that now.* "We had one drink and spoke about the trial he is principal investigator on." *Among other things.* "The receipts are already filed in the system should you wish to check. And besides, I believe the true love of his life is Arsenal. Pardon my bluntness, but I'm not going near that."

David lets out a derisive snort of laughter, shaking his head in amusement.

"Sienna, you truly are one of a kind. Look, I don't want you to think I believe any of this for a minute. I am merely letting you know what's about to hit you, so that you may be prepared. I intend to do all I can to help, but as company policies go, I unfortunately cannot prevent this altogether. You'll just have to ride it out."

Ride it out? Is he serious?

"You mean you just expect me to keep doing my job, as usual, while I am forced to go through this in parallel?" Disbelief soaks my voice. "You mean to say I should act like nothing has happened, while in between I am dragged off to legal hearings for something that is blown entirely out of proportion?" I cannot believe this is the same man who has encouraged me all this time, who trusted me despite my lack of experience, who repeatedly asks for my opinion on complex matters of scientific nature. It stings.

"That's exactly what I'm saying." His eyes are cold as they fixate on me, and as I back away, I realise this is not about me. It has never been about me. My knowledge is an asset, but only as long as I do not cause trouble. Anything that threatens to damage the company is a liability, and thereby expendable, and David Lewis would not think twice of letting me take the fall.

Walking home, I text John, stopping several times in the middle of the sidewalk to steady myself as my fingers keep shaking too much for the autocorrect function to handle. The full extent of what transpired only minutes ago is beginning to sink in, the implications overwhelming, and I suddenly cannot bear facing this alone.

That's ridiculous, comes his reply. **They will have to let it go, they don't have enough to make a case.**

So what should I do? I ask. **Do I need a lawyer or how does this work?**

It'll be internal hearings, right, so I assume you've got in-house counsel?

I don't know, I have no idea about these things. I am, I realise, silently freaking out.

To hell with texting, he's clearly on his phone. I press dial, but the tones ring empty. He does not pick up.

Well, a little hard for me to help without knowing details. Just bear with it, it'll be over before you know it.

That's it? That's how much fight he's putting up for me?

There's really nothing they can do to you with that accusation. You'll have to go through the procedures, but it'll come to nothing.

Nothing they can do to me? How about make me lose my job? Screw up my career? Or does that not count?

You've got this. I know you can handle it.

Yeah. I know it too. Like I handle everything else – on my own.

The moment I step inside my apartment, everything shatters. The keys fall out of my hand, crashing to the floor with an aggressive metallic clank, echoing in the hollow darkness.

I take a deep breath, resting my forehead against the door. Behind my closed eyelids, tears burn, unbidden, and for a moment, I am back in Ancona, in an empty hotel corridor during the small hours of night, with Nico's arms around me.

It's okay to be vulnerable sometimes.

Right now, my wildest fantasy is exactly that. Being held, and allowing myself to be vulnerable.

Chapter 19

Company policy? Like hell!" Rachel waves her hands in disgust over FaceTime. "He's allowing this to happen because he doesn't have the balls to step up and have your back like he ought to!"

Despite myself, despite everything, I smile. Watching her pace around the room, her resentment palpable, her jerky movements at odds with the soothing interior in the background, the combination of dark grey, white and pale birchwood straight out of a lifestyle magazine. In front of the two-and-a-half seat charcoal sofa, she comes to a halt, flopping unceremoniously onto it so that for an instant I am also treated to a phone-rendered view of her knitted socks as she pulls her legs up under her.

"Want me to come over with a scissor and make sure he doesn't ever reproduce again? Not that there would be much to cut, anyway." I suppress a snort. She always does manage to make me feel better, even in the darkest of moments.

"I think I just need to be alone for a while", I say. "Thanks for the offer, though. We could meet up next week, once I've managed to wrap my head around this a bit?"

"You know I'm here for you anytime, sis", Rachel says with empathy. "What did John say, by the way? Law is his area, after all."

"That it'll pass. That they don't have enough to make a case."

"That's good though, isn't it? I mean, he should know these things." She lies back on the sofa, her hair tumbling over the armrest and almost all the way to the floor. I do the same, stretching my legs.

"I suppose." I shrug. "I guess I just expected…" *More. More indignation, support, emotion, of some kind, on his part.* "I don't know, more of a reaction. It would make me feel infinitely better if I could be as certain as him that this is no big deal."

"He's at that golf weekend thing though, isn't he? Perhaps he just had a tough time getting away to talk in private."

"You don't think this is slightly more important?" Rachel gives me a look.

"You know I do. And I, for one, am, as previously stated, ready to murder the prick for you. For a handsome sum, naturally." She shifts the phone to her other hand. "My point is, don't be too hard on him."

I know her well enough to hear the unspoken addition in her voice, as if she was inside my head. *You always are.*

"I'll try", I sigh. "Anyway, thanks for the support. I'll see you soon, alright?"

"Take care of yourself", she says. "I mean it. This is complete bullshit, and you haven't done anything wrong. Don't let them get to you. Don't do anything I wouldn't do."

"Rachel, is there *anything* you wouldn't do?" I say, and at that she laughs, and continues to make ugly faces at me until I hang up the phone.

Staying put on the sofa, eyes pointedly away from my inbox and fixed on the TV, I work my way through a cooking programme where the participants repeatedly try and fail at properly making a soufflé; an obscure talk show I have never heard of before; double news reels adding up to at least one dead body dragged out of a tributary of the Thames, four gang-related shootings, two climate activist rallies blocking the traffic and one marijuana razzia in Croydon; a sitcom from Australia that must have been old when my parents were young; and, finally, a hard-earned victory for Milan in their final game of the year, at home against Lecce. Standing at nine wins and five draws, with only one loss thus far, they are vying for the top spot. I lean on my elbow, my chin in my hand, as I follow the post-match commentary.

"It's always nice to end the year with a win, but to be honest, I think we got lucky with this one", Nico says, relief in his voice as he kicks off his boots and pull off his socks. "They put up a bigger fight today than anyone of us anticipated, and that's always dangerous; you're at your most vulnerable when you're complacent. We've done it well so far; we're tied for the top spot in the league and qualified for the knockout rounds of the Champions League, but this is the easy part." He shrugs, continuing his analysis, and I can tell from his gestures that this has been bothering him for some time. "We came into the season well prepared and got off to a good start, but now other teams are finding their rhythms and catching up; come spring we'll have to prove what we're really made of, and judging from today, there is definitely still plenty of room for improvement", is his self-critical evaluation.

"You're pretty clear about what you want", the interviewer remarks. Nico nods, gesticulating to emphasise his point.

"Of course; within the team you must have a common goal, and it's always been important to me that the people around me share the same ambition. We had some new faces come in this season, but the younger guys have adapted well, and it will be useful for them to learn the ropes from us who have been around longer. Ultimately, we aim to challenge for all titles, so it's a matter of strategic planning and conserving our strength, because this will be a demanding stretch of the season and we need to do everything we can to give ourselves the best possible odds of success."

"So no wild parties over the Christmas break?" He smiles, shaking his head.

"No, there rarely are. It'll be quiet, with family. Although I daresay if my grandfather finds the grappa, there might be singing and possibly also dancing involved."

"That surely would be something to behold. *Grazie, Nico, e buon Natale.*"

"*Buon Natale.*" He shakes the reporter's hand, saluting him with a final "*Ciao*" as he disappears from view.

Merry Christmas, Nico, I think to myself, even as part of me wants to bang my head against the wall.

It is ridiculous. I have been casually watching this man for years, following his career, seeing him develop into the player he is today. Admiring his technical ability, his tactical sense, the fluidity in his movements, the accuracy of his passes. And now, here I am, wishing him Merry Christmas.

He's not just anyone anymore, I recognise. *He's not just a good player, he's a person.* If I am being honest with myself, I already knew more about him that first time than any of the people on the app Rachel forced on me, where I met John. I already had more reason to care before I knew the character behind the talent. I tilt my head back against the armrest of the sofa, deliberately harder than necessary. *Even so, you still need to move on.*

But every time I tell myself this, even in my head, it sounds less and less convincing.

Just before I turn off the lights, my phone flashes with a message. Groaning, I pull back the covers and glance at the screen, willing it not to be work-related. The entire painful charade in David's office is still fresh, the injustice and humiliation settling into a nauseating commotion in my stomach. Part of me dreads falling asleep, anticipating what my imagination will make of this and not particularly looking forward to the ensuing chaos of nightmares.

Thought you might like to see these before they're published, it reads. **Looking forward to hearing your thoughts. BR, Richard**

Suddenly, I am wide awake. He has attached a PDF file with a manuscript, and as I flip through the Phase II data, I can see where his and Professor McKenna's confidence stems from. Because the results are spectacular. As small as the sample size is, the rates of protection against severe disease and death are highly statistically significant, and safety looks promising. Even more exciting are the molecular patterns, where they, using conserved epitopes as immunisation targets, are able to detect antibodies reactive against both A and B RSV strains. There are no small children in the study, as would be expected, but the authors highlight that given the risk of severe illness in this age group, a childhood trial is already planned to be initiated following approval in adults.

Congratulations, I write back, purposely ignoring that it is now well past midnight. **This is ground-breaking.** And, feeling bold and rebellious, I add: **Let me know when you feel like another drink to discuss further.**

Chapter 20

The last-minute holiday rush hits me the instant I get off the train, people hastening past me, hurrying to get through their final Christmas shopping before the weekend. I get pushed back and forth along the bustling platform between scurrying mothers pulling along strollers and reluctant toddlers, suit-clad businessmen with their phones pressed to their ears as they type down notes for gifts dictated by their wives. The line of cabs usually parked outside the station is nowhere to be seen, and I decide to walk, as much for the breath of fresh air and open space after the crammed experience of the train journey as to clear my head. Normally, coming here, I would have preferred Mike to join me, a reliable buffer, there to push her words back, prevent them from reaching all the way into my heart. But this time, I feel a need to get away from it all, as much as to face things head on. Something in me knows I will have to, sooner or later.

Christmas lights in white, yellow, and blue, as well as the occasional stark red and green, adorn the balconies, binding the street together into a string of luminescent pearls. It is a walk of profound loneliness, in the cold darkness of the empty street, peeking in on the warm glow of candles from within strangers' homes; a melancholic movie scene, set to sombre music. From the outside, they all look happy, content, model families with exemplary, uncomplicated lives. But as I walk, I wonder how many uncomfortable secrets hide behind the impeccable Harvey Nichols curtains, how many heartbreaks and agonies and lifelong sorrows, how many wounds that do not heal and betrayals that cannot be forgiven.

My mother's house sits at the end of the lane, where it veers to the right to cradle the courtyard and the small park, diligently kept in a manner thoroughly British, it encompasses. A low brick wall runs the perimeter of the enclosure, its warm rusty colour mirrored in the houses; the sense of stability, of home, of preserved tradition on which the foundation of this country is built. Family is everything, every man's home is his castle. Except we are women, and none of us a princess, this house little resembling a home and even less a castle; it is more akin to a prison, guarding memories made in another place, another time.

She opens the door on my second knock, a cardigan pulled around her shoulders against the chill on the air, yet as usual, even though it is Saturday and she is home alone, her hair is neatly set, her pants ironed to perfection.

"Good to see you, darling", she says, greeting me with a tentative hug. I hug her back, more out of need for comfort from another human than a sincere will to be here. "Why don't you have a seat and I'll make tea."

The only time I drink tea is when I come here, as if this place is not so much part of my life as a temporary lapse into another astral plane. Firmly British, my mother believes in the healing power and irrevocable truths of tea more than the word of any man. Or so Mike says, at least.

"How is work?" she asks, placing cups and a pot of steaming hot water, bag of loose leaves protruding from the top, on the table. I laugh bitterly.

"Horrendous, thanks for asking." I tell her, in so many words, about what is coming, excluding the most offensive accusations and the gory details of legal procedures that I know she will not fully comprehend.

"And how are things with… John, is that his name?"

"Yes. Okay, I suppose." I shrug.

"You don't sound very enthusiastic."

"Should I be?"

"You were, once."

I shouldn't have been, and you should have made me see as much. I shake my head.

"Please let's not get into that again. You already told me they're having a baby. They seem perfectly fine without me." Still, I hear the bitterness in my own voice, can taste it, the sudden addition of a slice of lemon in the tea, and I grimace, setting my cup down. "You never did explain why you were so keen on Martin and I. Why you insisted, even though you knew what it would mean for me. For my career."

"I suppose I didn't." She takes a long sip of her tea, seemingly regarding the bottom of her cup, lost in thought. When she finally speaks, her voice is even, but her shoulders seem to droop forward, accepting defeat. "Before your father, there was another man in my life." I notice how she does not quite look at me. "He played the guitar like no one I've ever heard, writing his own songs. He had real talent. And he wanted me to come with him as he chased his dream." She sighs, readjusting the wedding ring she still wears, the bracelet that belonged to my grandmother she never takes off. "But I didn't. I was practical, and I stayed. Got myself a proper job, met a sensible, nice man who paid his rent and changed my tyres for me. Don't get me wrong, sweetie, I love you and your brother more than anything. I love your father too, in his own way. But sometimes, I just wonder what my life would have been like, if I had."

"Wow." For a moment, I am at a loss for words. The world revolves faster than usual, or maybe it is just me standing still, even backing away, unable to keep pace. "I just… Wow."

We sit in silence, the rapping of the old wooden clock the only sound, echoing the passage of time, the heartbeat of imprisoned memories, struggling to be free. In the end, I cannot stand it anymore. Pushing my cup away from me, over the table, I lean back in my chair, arms folded across my chest.

"You knew what I wanted, all along."

"Mike wanted to play football. That changed, too."

"And if there had been a girl, asking him to give it up and move to the countryside with her to tend sheep, would you have encouraged him to go then?"

Her silence is all the answer I need.

"It's not the 18th century anymore, you know. I can make my own way, be successful in my own right, without being judged on marital status alone." I hate the defensive tone in my voice, hate that we always end up here, stuck in this conversation. "Not everything I do comes down to whether or not I have a man to share it with." She tilts her head to one side, regarding me.

"No", she says, heaving a sigh. "I suppose not. But then again, it doesn't make you happy, either."

I am about to let fly, the usual tirade of how she has no idea what makes me happy, when a thought strikes me.

"Or was it more about me leaving? Me being too far away?" I think about her moving to Ipswich. I always assumed it was because of her job, but it only happened after both Mike and I left for university. *So that we could come stay more often*, she had said. Her only sister, cut off from her thanks to the irresponsible and irrational actions of girls too young to consider the consequences. For the first time, I wonder whether I have failed to see what my inconsolable pain and blind hatred brought upon others. "Were you afraid of being alone?"

"Not afraid", she says, but I sense I have struck a chord. "I guess I just couldn't quite bear the only family I had left dissolving. Not after I..." She falters, but I understand. *Not after I chose the way I did.*

I take it as my cue to leave, the remainder of my tea growing cold at the bottom of the cup. I get up, walking around to her side of the table. This time, I pull her in for a proper hug, hoping to convey with touch all that I lack the words to say.

On my way out, I turn back to her. She looks smaller, somehow, hands pulled into the sleeves of her cardigan, arms around herself as if for support. It is strange, the conflict of emotions that connects us. My anger and regret, her misguided attempt at turning back time.

"So how did you get over him? The guy you never followed?"

She laughs, then, that kind of short, almost desperate laugh that never sounds genuine and whose sole purpose is as a smokescreen, a diversion. There is sadness in her eyes when she looks at me, and a sort of resignation in her voice.

"Well, maybe I never really did. Perhaps that's my curse, to always be left wondering." She shrugs. "I guess we all have our demons, don't we?"

I will never allow myself to do that, I vow, in that instant. I think back on Rachel's words, late at night in Cotswolds. *You need to* allow *yourself to be over it. He can't be permitted to take this from you, too.*

No, I tell myself. *I will never be that girl. I need to end this. Be free of him, of them, once and for all.*

But the question is how. Would they speak to me if I called? And what would I even say, when it was them who wrought havoc on my life and not the other way around?

Even as I know it must happen, sooner or later, the mere idea makes me nauseous, the unpleasant anticipation of a poorly healed fracture being broken open and recast in order to eventually, finally, be whole.

Chapter 21

Please state your full name for the record."

"Sienna Elizabeth Archer."

"And is your residence currently in 46 Narrow Street, Victoria Wharf, London E14?"

"It is."

"I see here that you have prior entries in our registry."

"That would be speeding tickets."

"Several, by the looks of it."

"I'm sorry, how is this relevant?"

"Everything is relevant."

"Oh. Well, yes, I'm sure they're several. Do you want me to recount the dates and serial numbers of the cameras too?"

"Sarcasm will not be of any use to you here, miss Archer."

"No, I suppose it won't. That would require the receiving party to have a sense of humour."

The farce only begins at the end of January, adding to the absurdity of it all; any sense of urgency indicative of a severe offence diminished by the fact that holiday time takes full precedence. In a meeting room two floors below the office, a relic from another age that has somehow managed to escape restoration, the hearing is led by the corporate counsel, a portly man with a receding hairline and whose waistcoat might have been the right size two bypass surgeries ago. He coughs repeatedly, though whether to clear his throat or to remind the room of his presence remains unclear. He is flanked on either side by a taller man, all sharp angles and calculating eyes, his grey-streaked dark hair pristinely combed, and a woman, whose appearance brings to mind a bird, most prominently some form of vulture, her beaked nose buried in her laptop, her thin, long neck tied up in a high-collared brown dress that would have been too prude for a nun. She likely holds the role of secretary, continuously typing away at her keyboard, and seems to have made it her mission to look at me as little as humanly possible. On the rare occasion she does, her small, pale eyes are silently judging me from behind thick-rimmed spectacles.

It has all the amiable characteristics of a modern witch trial.

Without failure, they go through everything, from my basic work description to details of my scientific background, my daily routines and contacts, constructing a veritable pedigree of colleagues based on the frequency of our interactions. In their eyes, I am patient zero, carrier of a deadly and highly contagious disease, and they are to determine the degree of contamination, the damage already done to the community. I am astounded at the attention to detail, the level of scrutiny into the most mundane, remarks and arguments dating months back in time, the recollection of small, insignificant events that I had forgotten, which when put into a grander – and rather more skewed – perspective become far more sinister.

While I try my best to see John's angle, that it is groundless and will all come to nothing, I cannot help but worry, deep down, that this will come back to haunt me. That wherever I go, there will be records of this, and everyone will know, will judge, however much I defend my right. I could laugh at the hypocrisy of it all, how prejudices and injustices are abundant, and yet most people do not so much as bat an eye until the word is there on paper, like a signature etched in blood, a wax seal stamped in red across everything else. No one would touch my CV with a barge pole.

"In addition to the questioning, we'll have weekly assessments, as well as a final evaluation of your work performance before the summer", the belly pronounces, huffing. "At the end of May, we deem reasonable. To ensure there are no more", he looks at me pointedly, over the rim of his tiny, rectangular glasses, "mishaps."

Outstanding, I think, imagining the weeks stretching before me, days and days on end, this room at the very centre of my everyday existence, a repeat offender brought before his warder for his enforced weekly assurance that he will never do anything so despicable again.

The tall man glares, the vulture types. The room smells stale, of old pipe tobacco clinging to the walls and wool that has gone unwashed for too long, the dark wooden panels rendering the space gloomy and shrivelled, the shrunken space of a tomb gradually caving in.

I all but run from the room, slamming the bathroom door shut, retching until there is nothing left to disgorge but revulsion and shame.

Strangely enough, the rest of the world does not seem to notice that the ground I am walking on is no longer firm but fluid, a nasty form of quicksand so thick it appears solid, but which eventually, albeit painstakingly slowly, will inevitably drag you under. It revolves, as it usually does, and I am forced along with it, despite lacking all resolve and inspiration. I trudge on, through the muck of meltwater and grime that spill over the streets, my brain chasing itself in circles.

"Oh, one thing", John says as we are walking home one evening, behind us yet another dinner to take my mind off my weekly encounter with the jury of the underworld. He is back from Paris, and I cannot help but notice how we are both avoiding the topic, in the same manner we are avoiding talking about the hearings. He has not once asked how it is going, what is happening, and I am too exhausted to bring it up. The last thing I need is another confrontation. "They're changing the plumbing in my building. Bloody nuisance, but I suppose it must be done. Thing is…" He looks up, grimacing, his hands fiddling with the zipper on his jacket. "I won't have a functioning bathroom during that time. Nor kitchen, not that I use it much." He chuckles. "So I was thinking… Perhaps I could stay at your place, meanwhile?"

Stay with me? However underwhelming, the apartment is *my* space, my safe zone. I have not lived with anyone since Martin. Inwardly, I panic.

"I…" I begin, uncertain how to say no in as polite a manner as possible. *Can't he tell this is the worst possible timing?*

"Of course, it wouldn't be permanent. Just while they're getting it all sorted." But there is that hopeful look on his face again, the one that seems to tell me I need to come to his aid, even if he will not do the same for me. "But perhaps it could be good practice, you know, for the future."

For the future? We have barely uttered in so many words that we are a couple; it just seemed to happen, partly because there was nothing to outright refute it. Is this going to be the same? Time simply moving along, without announcements or milestones, riots or raptures, fading into a convenient grey everyday. The thought is terrifying.

"We'll make it work", he insists, taking my mollified expression for scepticism rather than alarm, and I have no answer to that but defeated silence.

He brings his belongings over the week after that; refurbishment work will not commence until March, he says, shoving his two large suitcases over the threshold and into the living room, but he might as well do it already now.

I take in his luggage with growing horror. *How much is he bringing? How long does he intend on staying?*

The sense of intrusion is reminiscent of what I felt when he came to visit in Cotswolds; the reluctance to accept this infringement of a space to which he has earned no right, the protective instinct not to yield what cannot be shared. Most of all, there is the feeling that he does not understand, does not notice the tender buds sprouting beneath his feet as he tramples along a path that he alone has decided on.

"You can use this, for your clothes", I say, motioning to one of the wardrobes I have, with effort, cleared for him. I glance at his suitcases, doubting it will be enough.

"And the rest?" he says, predictably.

"It's not a big apartment", I say. "You knew that when you packed."

"Yes, but…"

"I'll leave you to it", I say, deliberately moving away to give him space, though in reality it is mostly for me. The bedroom seems far too narrow, everything about it cramped in the face of accommodating twice its intended count.

Without warning, there is a crashing sound from the next room, the decisive clatter of broken glass on the floor. I hear him curse and consider for a brief second which way to turn – towards the apartment, or out into the corridor, out of this building.

Steeling myself, I walk into the living room and take in the sight of John grappling with a bottle of wine, the top chopped off into splinters, spread across the floor, the contents spilled across the front of his shirt, his trousers, pooling on the floor between his feet. His white socks, dampening by the moment, are flecked with red, an unseemly tinge to the combination of odours that settle over the room.

I watch silently as the stain spreads, the red soaking the pale grey carpet, blood from an open wound that refrains from closing.

"I thought we should celebrate", he says by way of explanation, the disfigured bottle still wet, tendrils of dark liquid dripping between his fingers and on to the floor.

"What", I say levelly, "are we celebrating? Not your non-existent plumbing, surely."

"Well, this, I suppose", he says, having at least the decency to look embarrassed. "Moving in, and all." He shrugs. "I just thought it'd be nice." He wrings his hands fretfully; twitchy, nervous movements with the bottle still in his hand. I think of Nico's smooth hands around the champagne bottle, secure, steady, delicate. I think about our toast, to nothing other than being alive.

"Moving in", I repeat, tonelessly. A deafening roar is rising inside me, the noise level increasing like that of an approaching hurricane.

"Don't worry, I'll clean up. I'm sorry." He looks around the kitchen. "Salt, that's the thing. Trust me, I've done this before." He starts flipping through my cupboards, and I feel something inside me reach a breaking point, the storm building to a crescendo. I cannot bear to be in this room, with him, for another second.

"You know what. Why don't you finish unpacking, and I'll go down to the laundry service by the station and ask if they have something stronger than that."

At night, I feel as though I am at the bottom of the ocean, the water heavy above my head, pushing down on my shoulders, suffocating, relentless, all-encompassing. Sleep is elusive, yet here I am, drowning, knowing full well it is a dream yet unable to resist as it pulls me under, time and time again.

Chapter 22

"These hearings are killing me." I sag into the chair opposite Rachel, reaching as if instinctively for the glass set before me.

Spring is flying by in a blur, and I have no idea what is going on. It feels as though I have not seen anyone for weeks. All I do is move, as if on a string, between the office and my apartment, choking out the hours at my desk only to, once done, continue in the sinister meeting room two floors down. I have not seen Mike in at least a month, Sean's enquiries about lab happy hours go unanswered, and I am sleeping my way through the weekends, much to John's dismay. At long last, my own part in the interrogation is over, but they leave no stone unturned, claiming there are still employees left to interview, though it seems at this rate even the janitors have been called up. According to corporate procedure, all the gory details will have to pass through the global head office before a verdict may be passed, meaning I still have to wait, and politely endure their smugness despite the urge to throw their words back in their faces. More than once, I have the distinct impression they are relishing this, their time in the limelight, an indecent form of satisfaction at their sense of power.

The one thing that keeps me going is the promise of Dr Richard Stevens, the data he shared after our last meeting, the contract he sent by personal delivery, wrapped in a thick envelope, the way one would treat a precious document of state. I have read it more times than I care to count, but it is still there, in its envelope, unsigned. Part of me is urging myself to do it now, to end this misery and be free, once and for all, but the other part, the rational, sensible part, knows I need to put this behind me first; I refuse to arrive at his doorstep with anything other than a spotlessly clean sheet.

"This is ridiculous. When did you last speak to your dickhead boss?"

"Let's see. It was before the recount of the internal conference last year, when Sonia started." These talks are the only reference I have, oblivious to the happenings of the outside world. "How long ago was that? Is it March, or April?"

"It's almost May. I'm worried about you."

Whatever happened to March? And April? I see the dimly lit meeting room before me, a dense centre of gravity, draining the life out of everything, even time itself.

"I thought it would be over by now? Didn't you say they had no more questions for you?"

"My colleagues are still being questioned, and most likely they'll find a way to speak to the rats in the basement too." Only yesterday Jasmine came back upstairs after her time on the stand, wrapping me up in a wordless hug. It is useless, keeping a lid on everything, not creating a scene, when everyone knows anyway. Rachel knows too, her face saying as much.

"I'm fine", I say; the world's oldest lie, the one everyone knows to mean you are most definitely not, and Rachel is nobody's fool. I let slip a deep, exhausted breath. "I just feel so alone."

"You're not alone, sweetie", Rachel says softly, her hand finding mine across the table. I yearn to snatch it away, but I do not. Because I love her, and I know she means well.

"The worst thing is, though I know I am right – I might not have been particularly diplomatic, but I was not wrong – they still manage to make you feel guilty. They interview everyone, and I mean everyone, from my closest colleagues to people who hardly know we coexist in the same building, and they bring up all these nasty little things, you wouldn't imagine. Every mistake you've ever made, every remark, every time you've lost your patience – everything is scrutinised, and you're judged, constantly, on things that have nothing to do with this whatsoever." I shudder. "You hear them read it out loud, and it sounds awful. Some of the things, even if you know they were meant as a jest, even though both of you laughed… It's torture." I look at her, suddenly afraid. "Am I really that horrible?"

"Si, you know you are not." She looks at me with something akin to sadness in her eyes.

"Do I just not care enough? Is there something wrong with me that I am this cynical person who just can't bring herself to bother? Who says whatever comes into her head, without heeding the consequences?"

"On the contrary", she says, eyeing me carefully. "You care too much. About everything."

I slump backwards in the chair, wondering whether to tell her I would not survive without her, or if that would worry her even more.

"How are things at home?" She does not take her eyes off me once, as if I am a mental liability, not to be trusted in open spaces and with sharp objects.

"They just are", I say, shrugging. "It's like we coexist in the same space but in two parallel realities. Only this past Sunday he got up early, saying we ought to go somewhere, I can't even remember, and was annoyed when all I wanted was to sleep."

"It's good though, isn't it, that he's trying to get you to think of something else?"

"True, but only as long as it's something he wants to do. I don't get it; either they expect you to be completely helpless, and can't deal with it when you aren't, or they leave you to handle everything on your own. There's no middle ground, it seems."

"Have you tried telling him this?" Rachel prompts. "He's not a bad guy, Si, he is just a man, and, let's face it, in many ways most of them are completely useless."

I lean over the table, burying my face in my hands.

"I think I'm going to buy a cat", I groan. "A black, fiercely protective kind that likes to bite useless men's balls off for kicks."

The one thing that does mark the passage of time are the elimination stages of the Champions League. Despite falling behind in the race for the league title, now likely to finish second behind local rival Inter, on the European stage Milan are seemingly possessed, storming through this year's tournament. After thrashing Porto in the round of sixteen, they proceed to promptly dispose of Bayern Munich, before narrowly scraping by against Liverpool in the semi-final. Nico is photographed holding his second Man of the Match award in as many games, and Rossi comments on how the club has not played at the highest level for many years, and how they are now back where they belong, competing for the big titles.

"We look forward to the final", he says. "This is the biggest game in club football, the one everyone wants to play, and, of course, win. We faced a tough draw, and we have shown that we are worthy of being here; being pushed to extra time and managing to score a late winner in the semis is a sign of mental strength, and we all grow from it as a team. I believe we are ready for the challenge."

It is already late when I find myself searching for statistics online, looking up the last Milan team that made the final rounds of the Champions League, the drama of the penalty shootout that won them the trophy, the star players of the last generation. Falling down a rabbit hole of detailed analysis of today's performance, I scroll further, finding a slow motion rendition of today's winning goal, Nico's brilliant assist that precedes it. A boisterous headline under "*Related*" catches my eye, and I click on it, despite myself, despite never reading tabloids.

"*Footballer separates from model*", it reads, in typical dramatic gossip fashion, and beneath there is a photograph, snapped with the targets caught unawares as they are leaving through the entrance to what looks like a grandiose luxury hotel, smartly shaped art deco door frames in black and gold set against white marble.

"*The couple was last seen together when attending the Serie A season awards...*" With her back to the camera, it is impossible to tell what she looks like; only Nico's silhouette is recognisable as he turns his head slightly to one side, his brow furrowing into a frown. I cannot help but notice he does not look particularly at ease, his hands at his sides rather than at her arm, walking half a step behind. My stomach turning on itself, I check the date of the article.

Over a year ago. Overcome with overwhelming relief, I release a breath I had not realised I was holding. Intrigued now, I keep reading.

"*The AC Milan star was both short and frank when asked about the split, stating that 'In the end, it turned out we wanted very different things, both out of life and out of this relationship'.*"

I wonder at all the things enclosed in a statement like that, the giant spaces between the lines. Did she let him down, or simply move on? My thoughts backtrack, as they often seem to do these days, when there is little else to brighten them, to that night, that day. *Why did you invite me in?*

Perhaps he was also getting over someone? Perhaps he was as lonely as I felt?

Suddenly I feel ashamed that I did not ask, that we never spoke about this. About her, about Nathan. About why we found ourselves in the situation we did. Two strangers, thrown together by fate, finding solace in each other.

It was more than that, though. Wasn't it? It must have been more.

The next link leads to a video clip from a similar flashy event, and before long, I find myself roaming YouTube, absorbed in footage from last year's UEFA awards' ceremony. Everyone who is anyone and their entourage are there, walking the gauntlet of photographers trying to outdo each other with larger-than-life objective lenses. My stomach lurches involuntarily as Nico emerges on the red carpet, the fit of his suit immaculate. *Of bloody course it is.* An image of John's loose fit button-up shirt comes unbidden into my head, and I groan. Part of me feels terrible; I should not be doing this. Then he turns, smiling, and my insides do another backflip. He is waving to someone off camera, and I wonder impatiently who it is, until I see a woman emerge, her hair raven-black, the back of her dress low-cut to reveal Mediterranean olive skin. Her step has that natural, typically Italian flair that women from the northern hemisphere could never even hope to achieve, every movement seemingly perfectly choreographed to enhance every curve, every lock of shining hair. I bite my tongue to hold back the scream of frustration within, until I see him kiss her on both cheeks, then hold out his hand to a man appearing behind them, a girl of about six or seven in tow. She looks a bit shy, her hand disappearing into that of her father's as she stays close to his imposing shape. Nico crouches in front of her, a smile on his face, arms spread wide. And of course, she cannot resist. The way he holds the little girl does something to me I cannot explain; the tenderness in his touch, the affectionate expression on his face. I watch him plant a kiss atop her head and lift her up, perching her on his hip, promptly proceeding to give interviews in this fashion. In the background, the parents are smiling. I realise the woman must be his sister, Flavia, with her family; her husband, the dentist, their daughter Alicia. I feel a sudden urge to Google their parents, because with this level of genetic lottery success, I would be surprised if they had not already won a real one.

Tearing my gaze away, my eyes alight, as if by either chance or design, on the top shelf in the kitchen, a brown paper bag protruding from its wooden rack. Pulling myself up, I grab it, crumbling the wrinkled bag in my hand as I remember the accommodating waiter, the cash payment, the magnificent vista of the setting sun behind us.

I look at the wine bottle, its elegantly rounded neck, the small boutique winery's circular logotype etched on the front, wondering if I should dare open it. Whether it will be as good as I remember, or whether it is merely a figment of my imagination, a fantasy

I willed so hard to be true I projected it on an innocent bottle of wine. Whether it will release a flood of memories I am not certain I can handle, which probably ought to be left well alone, but that I know I will always cherish in my heart, or whether I have imagined it all in a dreamlike state of delusion and the wine is actually nothing more than cheap trash that will ruin the dream altogether.

I watch it intently for a while, thinking of the orchids, the hearings, the stained carpet, the trip to Paris.

Fuck it.

With one swift moment, I rip the top cover, and before I have time to stop myself, the cork is out. A scent of exotic blossoms, of southern heat, of ripe peaches, of elderflowers grown by the seashore, waft over me, and I feel myself sinking to my knees by the sofa table, my nose buried in the glass my trembling hands are cradling the way a starving man would the piece of bread he has just been given by a pitying passer-by. I feel tears burning behind my eyelids as the taste of saline and faint traces of vanilla grace my tongue, and by the time John opens the door and drops his briefcase on the floor, I am halfway down the bottle and openly crying, because it is beautiful. It is all so beautiful, and so very far out of my reach.

Chapter 23

The last weekend of May, the Champions League final. AC Milan against Real Madrid. It does not get much bigger than this. The last evaluation meeting finally past me, I feel like celebrating, even though I, despite their reluctant admittance that there were no additional remarks, do not quite dare hope I have seen the last of our voluminous counsel and his charming goons until concluding judgement arrives.

Yet I find myself at home, by myself. John is golfing, Rachel and Tom have gone to visit his parents in Bristol for his mum's birthday. Mike is watching the game with his old teammates, and the last thing I wish to do is act the poor little sister who did not have any friends of her own to meet. Considering the apartment, I decide against staying in. For the first time in weeks, months, I feel my spirits lift as I step out into the street, into the tentative sunlight of approaching summer. The horror might be over at last, and it is as if I can breathe again, a heavy rock lifted off my chest that puts a sudden spring in my step as I walk, aimlessly, along the waterfront, relishing the warmth edging into the air and the promise of freedom.

The bar I find is one I previously have not noticed, most likely disappearing into the background blur of old storage buildings. Today, however, its pale-yellow brick walls are covered by flags and scarves, banners stretching the entirety of the open square in front, where tables are already full, waiters struggling to clear beer glasses at a rate at least approaching that with which they are emptied.

I squeeze myself inside, finding a seat by the bar, ordering a beer for the atmosphere and following the warm-up and pre-game analysis with interest. Despite my overall sense of sudden, welcome ease, I realise I am nervous. I know what this victory would mean to Nico, for his entire career. I feel, in my gut and in my heart, how much I wish for him to win it, to see him lift that holy grail of a cup towards the night sky. And, perhaps because of all that has happened in the past months, perhaps because I am finally done lying to myself, I allow myself to embrace it. As the band and performers file out from the pitch after the opening act and the players take their positions for the anthem, the beer is already gone, my hands gripping the seat and my tongue stuck between my teeth as I watch the drama unfold.

The game is tense, both teams playing with less flair and more focus than they have done earlier in the tournament, the stakes and nerves of the final apparent on both sides. Rossi and his German colleague in the Milan defence are kept constantly alert, the attacks coming at high frequency, though not as lethal as they have been in previous games. The midfield is a battleground, evenly balanced on all positions, the fine-tuned elegance normally permeating their game decomposed into a rough, unyielding positional war.

The stalemate endures until the eightieth minute, when Nico receives the ball in open space, his opponent tight on his heels. He moves left, shifting the ball with one touch, then attempts to turn, to lose his shadow, and without even seeing his face, I know he knows, sense it in his body language, already before the Real Madrid midfielder feints to the right to escape with the ball, that this was it, the opportunity they have been waiting for.

And in that split-second opening, the whites do not hesitate. They pounce, like wolves scenting blood, and in a moment in time that lasts less than ten seconds but feels like a stretched-out, slow motion eternity, I watch the ball slip through the Milan goalkeeper's hands and into the net.

Next to me, a girl screams, the instant before the bar erupts, in equal amounts of groans and cheers, as my world crumbles. *Or, well, not really mine so much as Nico's.* But I feel as though it might as well have been mine, with my ambitions being flattened to dust, my dreams slipping like sand through my fingers.

I turn to look at her, realising I have been so absorbed by the game it is the first time I have noticed she is there. Her face covered by her hands, all I can make out is a mop of red hair, her slim shoulders shaking in what I can only assume to be sobs. Then she catches me looking, and, removing her hands, waves them around, sniffling ungraciously.

"I'm sorry", she croaks, her voice slightly hoarse. Seeing the most likely desolate look on my face, she shakes her head. "I really didn't mean to offend, I just got so carried away. Geez, this really is doing nothing for my nerves." She waves a waiter over, chatting him up in a familiar manner. "I'll need another glass of wine to cope with this. Yes, the same one will do just fine. The Pinot Noir, yes. No, not the one on the list, the one Mark has open at the back. Thanks a lot." Leaning forward, around him, she glances at me. "What about you? Let me buy a glass. The Chardonnay is excellent."

"I..." I begin, but before I can object the waiter is off, and the girl has scooted closer along the bar.

"It's the least I can do", she says, waving away my feeble objection. She glances at the match clock. Four minutes of injury time, and I can tell she really needs that drink. "Besides, I think girls like us ought to stick together, even if we're on different teams, don't you think?"

"Girls like us?" I cannot help but smile, and she shrugs, suddenly self-conscious.

"You know, going out to watch football on our own." She rolls her eyes. "Because it's too important to miss out on, too tragic to watch at home by yourself, and no one was able to join. Plus, you might need a drink or two to stay calm. Correct?"

She is so spot on I have to laugh, and the waiter chooses that exact moment to appear with our drinks. The redhead throws him a brilliant smile and whispers something in his ear, hand on his elbow, and buries her slightly pointy nose in the wine glass. Amused, I sniff my own drink, subtle hints of oak blending with notes of white flowers.

"Good, eh?" she says, still swirling. "The floral notes are exquisite; I love how they've worked with the minerality in it without overdoing the oak."

I take a sip and cannot help but nod.

"Catch that faintest hint of something lactic on the tip of your tongue?" she goes on. "Like the whiff of a newly opened jar of yoghurt. It's partly due to the style of winemaking, how they let the acids develop, but also because it's still so young; some of it will settle with age, but I personally like them like this, I think it's quite unique."

"You really know your stuff." I thought I was somewhat into wine, but this girl is clearly leagues ahead and has just effectively exposed how much I did not even know that I did not know. She offers me a shrewd smile.

"Well, if someone ought to know, it would be me, otherwise I would be very bad at my job." I raise a questioning eyebrow.

"I'm in wine import." She shrugs. "Sommelier by training, but I like to go to restaurants, not work in them. So I basically make sure to supply all my favourite places with my favourite wines." She winks. "Though my dream combination still seems it has some way to go. I want to open a really good wine bar that also shows sports. A classy sports bar, if you like."

"I thought you didn't want to work in restaurants."

"Oh, I know! It mostly *sounds* romantic, doesn't it? But I'd love to hang out in one, and if there won't be any without me opening it, then I guess it'll just have to be me to do it."

I wince inwardly at the way I have been reasoning with myself, about my need for stability, the fear of stepping out into the unknown. Her eyes gleam mischievously. "Good thing is, I can always claim I'm doing a customer visit." She smiles, raising her glass, and I feel a stab of jealousy. I wish I was able to just go for what I wanted that way, and in the same instant wonder what is holding me back. Frowning, I turn my eyes back to the screen, hiding my thoughts behind my glass. The girl leans across, conspiratorially.

"Can I tell you a secret? I'm not really all that crazy about the rest of the team, but I'm really into this because one of the players." She sighs elaborately. "I know, such a cliché, right? But I just love his work ethic, his passion for the game, his leadership. I still remember the first time I watched him play, and now I can't stop watching. Silly, right? I guess I just want him to be happy and successful."

Something constricts in my throat, as I think of my feelings before the game, my instant reaction at the goal.

"Actually, it's the same for me", I manage. I have no intention of providing details, but I do relate to what she says. "I love to watch Nicolo Di Luca. It's something with his technique, it's just so effortless. And then he does something incredible, and it just looks so easy."

For a moment she looks me over, and I pray she will not see anything there that will give me away, but she delivers yet again.

"Excellent choice, my dear. His first touch", she makes a 'chef's kiss' kind of gesture with her fingers to her lips, "is immaculate." Her choice of words is so unfortunate I have to look away, but she does not seem to notice. "And, let's be fair, he's not bad to look at, either."

"To be honest, I didn't think about that at all, at first", I say. "I just saw him play and was hooked. But, well, the more I watched…" *There we go, understatement of the year.* She grins at me, and I shrug.

"Great minds think alike. Did we just become friends?" I laugh, and it is refreshing and relieving and wonderful.

"It doesn't look any better", I smile.

"I'm Ali." She sticks her slender hand out, the zippers on her black leather jacket jingling. Underneath, she wears a white shirt, the golden Madrid crest occasionally visible as she moves. A plain gold chain with a single diamond hangs around her neck, harmonising with the jersey. *How to turn your match wear into an accessory.* "Or really, it's Alanna, but that's a bit much for me. My parents were going through a mutually obsessive *Black Velvet* phase, so Mrs Myles is firmly on my shitlist ever since. Being named after a one hit wonder isn't all it's made out to be."

"Sienna." I grab her hand in return. "After… no one, I guess?" I do not think I have ever asked.

"Good for you." Ali leans back, shaking her hair out of her face. "Always be yourself. Unless you can be a medieval town in Tuscany, then definitely be that." I cannot help but laugh. Ali's no-nonsense attitude is delightfully entertaining.

On impulse, I find myself asking:

"So, my friends and I are going to the Euro final and have a ticket to spare. Do you fancy joining?"

Her eyes widen, then lit up as if illuminated from within.

"Are you kidding?" she croaks. "No way."

"Way", I laugh, echoing Mike's response to me, almost touched by her honest shock. "Seriously, I've already exhausted my friends' circle when it comes to football interest, and it's my brother's friend who's been put on probation by his fiancée." I shrug. "It'd be great with another female voice of reason."

"Gosh, you're killing me." She puts a hand over her heart. "I'd love to. Like, you have no idea how much. I'm in. I'll be there. What do I owe for the ticket? And do you already have some place to pre-game? Or could I possibly help with that?"

"I suppose we'd either be at mine or my brother's, but we really haven't planned that far. I'm sure we're open to suggestions."

“There’s a great place close to Wembley, a friend of mine works there. Great Italian wine list, plenty of beers on tap for those so obliged.”

“Sounds perfect”, I say. We shake on it, clinking our glasses as we exchange phone numbers. Although it is such a trivial thing, a conversation in a bar, a connection made, an invitation, it awakens something inside me. A part of me, reckless and craving adventure, stirs, as after a long hibernation. I realise Rachel was right to worry; it has been a long time since I was truly myself, and I despise how I have allowed this enervation to leech so far into my soul.

“Are you seeing anyone?” Ali drags me back to the present.

“Actually, I am.” It still feels strange to say it. “Since about eight months.” *So why does it still not feel like we truly know each other?*

“So why isn’t he here tonight? Doesn’t he like football?”

“Not really. Well, apart from the Sunday Premier League pub.” I shrug. She wrinkles her nose, as if personally offended.

“Girl, seriously. You need to teach him the important stuff.”

“I guess”, I say, though I do not mention how I have deliberately separated those two parts of my life. I wince as I remember that in a little over a month’s time, they will be brought together. “He’s coming to the final, so hopefully that’s a good place to start.”

“Let’s hope so.” She suddenly rolls her eyes. “Look at us. This conversation certainly wouldn’t pass the Bechdel test, would it? First footballers and now this.” She shakes her head. “New topic. Tell me, what do you do for a living?”

Later that evening, I watch the post-match interviews, the gloom of the deserted catacombs beneath the stadium a glaring contrast to the fireworks of the sparkling celebration still ongoing on the pitch. Here, away from the spotlight and the glory, the backdrop of concrete and loss is even more pronounced, the blow even harder felt.

He looks so dejected it pains me to watch, but I still cannot tear my eyes away from the screen. His voice is flat, strained, and tired, yet professional. No sign of his usual humour, his light-hearted smile. This is different from the focused and determined Nico of the press conference before Christmas, different from the playful, relaxed, sociable Nico I know. Until now, I have not fully realised to what extent I have gradually learnt to recognise his moods and gestures, relating to his joys and agonies, coming to understand a man whom I have only briefly met, even though he may in some ways know me better than almost anyone else.

"Against a team like this, you don't get many opportunities. And you need to make the most of the ones you get, because they can turn the tables on you in an instant. Today, we didn't take our chances, but they did, and that made all the difference." He sighs, and I can tell he wants to be anywhere but here. "Obviously, this is not how I wished for this evening to go. This was, by far, the most important game of my career, and I don't need to tell you how disappointing it feels to see that chance slip away. I made a fatal error, and for that I can only apologise, to our supporters, and to everyone who came out here today to watch. But the truth is", he takes a deep breath, and I can see this requires effort, sour admittance from damaged pride, "they were better today. They beat us, fairly, and they deserve this victory, however bitter it may taste for us."

"So what's next? How do you recuperate from this?"

"We have a couple of days to regroup", he says, exhaling slowly, the mere idea a struggle. "Then we meet up with the national team and head for England."

England.

Of course, I have known it this whole time, but only now is it starting to sink in. I sit paralysed, staring at the screen.

He is coming here. He's coming to England.

So close, yet so far away.

Chapter 24

The championships are upon us before we know it, the flags, banners, crowds, and fan zones exploding throughout the countryside as thousands of supporters from all over Europe gather to support their teams. London's streets are brimming with colour, men and women, young and old, friends, couples and families descending on the city like a swarm of joyful locusts, proudly flaunting their nation's jerseys. On every street corner, a particular pub has taken upon itself to be the meeting point for a certain country's fans – as I walk home from the office, I encounter not only the red and white of the English – who, naturally, are everywhere – but also multiple renditions of the blue of the French, the black of the German and the red and yellow of the Spanish, the four main favourites to the title, if one is to judge by media coverage. Out of nowhere, spring has exploded into summer, and on the back of a wallowing heatwave outdoor terraces and pub yards are packed, seemingly around the clock, as if the promise of sports and sun has made everyone forget there is also a reality to be dealt with.

According to tradition, Mike and I follow the events closely, an A3-size printout of the draw taking up residence on his refrigerator door. We bet on the results of each competition round in our usual fashion – the loser buys the drinks for the next game. After the group stages, I am firmly in the lead, but Mike is gaining on me, having dropped his pretence of studying head-to-head statistics after a few miserable calls and now going purely by feel, resulting in him nailing surprise wins for Czech Republic against the Netherlands and Sweden versus Switzerland. Following the former, Rachel calls me so I can hear Tom's uncharacteristic yelling in the background; his very distant Czech ancestry seemingly having emerged at a strategic moment.

"I have no idea what's gotten into him", she gasps as we laugh over the phone at his victory dance, fuelled by a large pint of Czech beer, until our bellies ache. "He never does this."

"Pray for Czech Republic to reach the final, then", I say, though I know it is highly unlikely as they are set to play Spain next, "because that would most definitely be a sight."

There are days when I hardly see John at all; despite the reconstruction in his building being completed, he always seems to find new things he has forgotten in my flat, or one reason or another to stay over, and I neither have a valid excuse for him not to, nor the energy to constantly argue. I sense the time is nearing when I must come to a decision: either push him away forcefully, or give in altogether, and spending as much time as I can out of the apartment gives me a much-needed respite from thinking.

Predictably, England plays all their group stage matches at Wembley, rendering the team an enormous home field advantage with ninety thousand at their backs. Even come the knockout stages, the crowd support is apparent, and you have the distinct feeling this might truly, finally, be their year. The draw is favourable, too, with the likes of Denmark and Sweden in their bracket rather than more prominent favourites such as France or Germany, who are squaring off already in the quarterfinals. I notice, though, how there are others, dark horses moving on the outskirts of everyone's attention, those lacking the blockbuster names and the Hall of Fame coaches, but who are discreetly edging their way closer and closer to the ultimate goal. Italy breeze through the group stages undefeated, scoring a total of eight goals along the way, which must surely be a championship record, but it only warrants a short paragraph on the back page of the morning news.

Hungary have done well, while Belgium have been underwhelming; far from everyone can handle the pressure, and despite successful club spells, many players struggle to find their rhythm, effectively demonstrating how international football is something else entirely. There are upsets and walks in the park, aggressive fouls and faked injuries, humbling routs and spectacular last-minute comebacks, managers getting hostile on the sidelines; there is flair and finesse and brute force, jubilation and heartbreak; all the drama, and then some, exactly the way a championship is supposed to unfold.

As June draws to a close, Mike and I open the doors to his balcony wide, letting the evening sunshine and the warm winds of summer in as we watch Italy beat Spain in the semi-finals at Old Trafford in Manchester. It is a tactical masterclass display from start to finish, and despite a late Spanish goal off a set-piece that sends them to extra time, there is never truly any doubt; Italy have been the better team all evening.

And as I refill our glasses, I glance at Mike's homemade drawsheet and realise, as he diligently fills it in, that England will play Italy at Wembley for the European Championship, and instantly know two things.

I will be there, and I will not be supporting England.

Lying in bed, I scroll through the feed on my phone. All of a sudden, there it is: a post. The entire Italian team depicted as they raise their linked arms in salute to the fans, the red and brick backdrop of Manchester United's home stadium framing their celebration. **Next stop Wembley!** the caption reads, pride and excitement unmistakable in those few words, all the way through screen and wireless.

He has not posted much, I notice, and nothing since the Champions League final. Perhaps it is superstition; perhaps it means nothing at all. Before that, there are pictures from training, Nico and Federico Rossi goofing around, their smiles easy, relaxed, comfortable. They give nothing away, no clue as to what goes on in his head. A sense of revenge, a need to prove himself? An uncertainty he cannot quite shake off, that when it truly matters, he does not have what it takes? Regardless of the scarcity of information, the immaterial emptiness of digital files, this is the closest he has been for months.

I look at the *Send message* button on his profile. Should I just? But he will almost certainly never read it, will probably not even notice it among all the other spam messages people like him receive. *And what if he does?* I ask myself. Is it worse to cling to a delusion for too long, or to have the dream shatter in your face?

Hey, I write, self-conscious to the bone. *Hope you remember me.* But I cannot bring myself to type it down. **Good luck in the final! Hope you enjoy London.** And then, after a deep breath, I add: **If you hear someone cheering too loudly for Italy – ergo facing immediate deportation – from Level 1 of the south end stands, it might be me.**

My finger hovers over the *Submit* button for what feels like the time elapsed from the Big Bang up until this very moment.

When I finally force it down, I immediately close my phone and throw it far away from me.

In the remaining days before the final, I see his name in the list of messages, moving further and further down as other texts fall into my inbox. Most likely he has not even seen it, what with the thousands of random messages he must get every day. I read somewhere that public personas with a verified profile can only receive communication from other people with the same type of account, but I do not know if that is true. I am not on social media enough to know these things, and I do not bother to find out. I tell myself that it is fine, that it does not matter.

But the one thing I will not do is to check whether the message has been read or not.

Chapter 25

The bar Ali recommended is making a roaring business on the day of the final, the outdoor tables brimming over with occupants, some simply standing with their beers in hand, leaning against the brick wall or wooden fences that surround the seating area. A queue has already formed at the door, but Ali, seeing us arrive, bursts forward, waving us in, past the line, much to the loud displeasure of those left behind.

"So good to see you!" she calls, throwing her arms around me. "I'm so excited, I still can't believe this! Thanks so much again for inviting me. I don't quite know how I can repay it, but I'll do my best. So everything in here is on me tonight and I have Alex's" – she waves at the dark-haired guy behind the bar, who looks up from polishing glasses to give us a nod and a smile – "personal promise that he'll open just about anything you might wish for."

"Thanks a lot, Ali", I say, hugging her right back. "That's far too kind of you. So glad you could join us!" I indicate to the others. "Guys, this is Ali, the reason we're having this amazing warm-up going on. Ali, this is my brother, Mike; my closest friend, Rachel, her husband Tom, my boyfriend John."

"Nice to meet you all." Ali shakes their hands, one by one, smiling. "Ali Hewitt."

"Quite a place, this", John says, looking the bar over, the clash between old factory walls and the interior of a river steamer, complete with beer on tap drawn directly from the brewery in the basement through a massive black metal pipe. It is certainly not his usual scene, but I sense he is reluctantly impressed.

"Yes", Ali nods, "isn't it great? Alex and his brother bought this when they were just out of sommelier and cookery school, respectively – Alex and I studied together –, they'd had their sights on it for ages but had to save up, even though at that time it was a complete dump. The roof caved in, the windows falling apart..." She gestures at the high ceiling, the raw timber rafters. "And just look at it now. They had a vision, and it really came through spectacularly."

"I love it", Rachel says, fingering the bar chairs, rustic yet graceful in their simplicity. "And the drinks are good." She raises her glass, as if it was not obvious what she was referring to. "So, what did you call this one again?"

"The domain is called Taurasi, which is one of the most respected regions for the production of wines made from the Aglianico grape." The memory pinches at my heart; all these tiny reminders, sharp like shards of broken glass.

"Barolo of the south, was it?" Mike interjects with a smile. I raise an eyebrow, but do not say anything, and Ali nods, enthusiastically.

"Exactly!" she exclaims. "It is quite similar to both Nebbiolo, which is used to make Barolo wine, and Sangiovese, which dominates in Tuscan Chianti wines, but this area is so much smaller and less well-known, it often flies under the radar." She gestures over to the bar. "Alex always had a thing for Italian wine, I think he buys pretty much everything he sees that is good. This place has a huge cellar, beneath our feet, where all the goods are stored."

I whistle, impressed, and move to refill my glass. After all, it is Italy we are watching tonight, and I know at least one Italian with a particular connection to this very grape. *Perhaps it will bring him luck.*

Out of the corner of my eye, I catch Mike throw an appreciative glance at Ali, and lean closer to whisper something in her ear. She laughs, and a warm feeling settles in my stomach.

England is the home of many an impressive stadium, but the walk up to Wembley surpasses them all, the sight of the proud national arena with its domed white arc shining brightly as it reflects the sunlight, a beacon to the nation. We are moving in a heaving sea of white and red, the blue banner of the Three Lions fluttering above our heads, the way I imagine knights once upon a time would have brandished the arms of their lords and kings. The crowd is singing, teeming with excitement, and I can almost feel my nerves crawling out of my body and settling on the outside of my skin.

The English press is predictably overconfident, not missing a chance to point out that while many of the Italians have performed well this year, they have always fallen short of the big trophies; most prominently, Nico and Rossi, with Milan, missing out on both the league title and the Champions League in the very last games of the season. Moreover, it has been a long year, with matches all the way up until two weeks before the Euros; they must surely be tired, worn out, mentally detached. The team captain, Leonardo Selmi, is aging; he will not be able to handle the brute physicality of the English team. One can practically smell the victory they have already bestowed upon England in the printing ink coming off the page, and I sense it all around me as we walk up the stairs to our seats, the expectation, the tension, the taste of long-awaited glory quivering in the air, the story already written: the home tournament with the fairy-tale ending. I tug at my shirt, my clothing in itself a small act of defiance. At a glance, the red does not stand out from the rest of the crowd, but around my neck, I have draped a thin black scarf, the overall combination subtly representing the colours of Milan.

The stands arch high above our heads, the noise level reaching a crescendo as it is time for warm-up, the minutes finally ticking down to the climax of the tournament.

To a deafening roar, the players come out, and my stomach lurches at the sight of him; after all this time, despite all the hours in front of the TV, this is somehow the ultimate verification that he is truly real, and not, after all, a figment of my imagination. He exists, and he is here, so close to me that I can see the way his hair moves as he runs, notice the way his palms rub along the grass as he bends to tie his laces, follow his eyes as he takes a measure of the stadium, the height of the stands, the sheer amount of spectators milling in like ants into a hill, the gradual build-up of match day intensity.

So close, and yet he has no idea that I am here, watching his every step. No way of knowing how I am, in this very moment, willing him to turn, to look at me, to somehow, impossibly, notice me amidst the ocean of unrecognisable faces. A part of me wants to shout, to wave, to call out to him, to let him know that I am there. Why I am there.

He didn't reply to your message. Even if he knows you're here, it won't matter. But I still cannot tear my eyes away, or ignore the hollow sense of longing in my chest.

Mike enthusiastically points out the English left-winger, a prodigy who is already being labelled the next big thing, and the goalkeeper, who both saved and scored a penalty in the semi-final win over Denmark, but all I see is him, my eyes constantly diverted, as if he is the only person in the stadium, all ninety thousand reduced to a background blur, his contours the only ones in focus.

As the players line up for the national anthems preceding kick-off, Ali leans over, whispering in my ear:

"I guess you're not really an England supporter today, are you?" She smiles, knowingly, and I shake my head, grinning in a *sorry-not-sorry* fashion. The girl does not miss a beat.

From the start, the game is fast-paced and physical. My eyes follow Nico as he dodges, feints, is challenged but stays on his feet, keeps running. Somehow, he finds the angles, the openings, the opportunities that no one else seems to anticipate, or even perceive. He has been brilliant all season, with a few critical exceptions, but this might be the best I have ever seen him. He is floating, barely touching the ground, moving with cat-like grace, pouncing on the ball with the acuity of a predator, leaving nothing to chance. The level of concentration is apparent in every movement, his face a mask of determination, the world shrunk to the tunnel vision of the ball, the goal, and the positions of his teammates. It is as if he is playing all by himself, dancing across the pitch to a tune only he can hear, everything else filtered out and forgotten.

Italy take the lead early, much to the dismay of the home crowd, after a sublime effort by winger Antonio Costa, playing the ball in behind the English defence to open goal for forward Matteo Bianchi. Just before the break, England equalise after a controversial penalty; there are several players in the box, duelling for the ball as the corner kick comes in, and whether there is a handball on Rossi is difficult to see in the commotion. Loud whistles follow the English forward as he raises his fist towards the Italian section of the stands after his equaliser, and the pressure reaches boiling point. After that, though, it is 1-1 at half-time, at sixty minutes in, at seventy-five; both teams increasingly tired, irritated, desperate, the promise of eternal glory so infuriatingly close, yet so agonisingly far away.

A rough challenge on Leonardo Selmi sends the Italian section of the crowd into a frenzy as he twists on the ground, holding his ankle, clearly in pain, all the while the English defender shakes his head and proclaims his innocence, protesting wildly.

The referee blows his whistle and gestures to a point right in front of his feet, and the stadium roars from catcalls and boos. The Italians huddle together, clearly arguing over who should take the free kick – my heart is beating far too fast as I watch Nico walk up to the spot, looking the distance to the goal over, sizing it up, as if performing a complex engineered calculation of the path the ball must travel.

You are *good with numbers.*

I cannot hear anything over the noise; it is akin to being in the midst of a raging hurricane. The English team gathers in the box, the goalkeeper yelling instructions – the Italians crowding them, the scuffling and shouting, elbows shoving to create space where there is none.

I see him release a breath, shrugging his shoulders as if trying to unwind, to find that place where the ball becomes an extension of himself. Then he takes two steps back, aiming, and I can barely watch, my breath caught in my throat, my hands shielding my eyes.

In the end, I do not see it go in. I hear it. Hear it in the way his shoe slides over the leather, in the rush of air as it flies in a bent course over the heads of the wall, in the metallic bang as it skims the crossbar, the final rattling of the net as it is diverted away from the goalkeeper's reaching hands, and, ultimately, the eruption of the stadium as if an earthquake has suddenly devoured all of north London.

And I do not even think, I just react – in an instant I am on my feet, out of my seat, running down the stairs to lean over the railing, my hands in the air and my throat hoarse from screaming, my eyes nowhere but on that single figure on the pitch running, as if in slow motion, his arms raised, towards this end of the stands. I have no way of knowing whether he sees me, but I do not even care; I keep jumping, keep screaming, beside myself, and all of a sudden, he is there, climbing the rafters, and too late I realise that it is for me. Then his arms wrap around me, and his mouth finds mine and as if by reflex my tongue reaches for his, and beneath half-closed eyelids I glimpse that flicker of recognition, that teasing smile, and it aches within just how much I have missed this. As if by their own accord, oblivious to all around them, my hands weave themselves into his hair, his hands around my waist, my neck, and I do not ever want this to stop, I have waited far too long… And then, with a wink, he is gone, back on the pitch, as unreachable as the rest, fleeting ants running by far below my elevated feet. And I feel the delayed blush heating my cheeks as I turn around, thousands of eyes in the stands rushing to meet mine, whispers as loud as air raid sirens, and their looks as I make my way back to my seat – surprised, scandalised, amused, but none of them seeing this for the homecoming it actually is.

"Boy, did he take some liberties", John scoffs. "Are you okay?"

And I can barely nod, my insides still swimming, my eyes desperately trying to focus on something, anything, that will not give them away, not now, but Rachel still sees. I see her eyes widen, her mouth open, her hand reaching to cover it, and even as I shake my head, I hear her say:

"Oh… so it was *him*, wasn't it?"

And John turns to look at me, without comprehending, but also with suspicion, because there is no way I can hide the heat rising up my throat, into my face, no way I can conceal the flush of my skin or the smile on my face. He knows, without actually knowing, that something is amiss.

"Him, who?" he says, and Rachel's eyes grow wider.

"He doesn't know?" she mouths, which makes things even worse, and yet, all I can think of is how well we fit together, how my entire being has seemingly waited to feel this way once again, with him.

After the final whistle, after the celebrations, when the crowds start to mill out, I hang back, uncertain why. While the others head for the exit, I randomly stuff my scarf beneath a seat, calling to Rachel even as she turns around to see what the heck I am doing.

"You go ahead! I just need to find my scarf; it should be here somewhere." I gesture vaguely at the floor, beer cans kicked aside, caps flung to the ground in anger. "I'll catch up, it'll only be a minute."

Whether or not there is something knowing in her eyes, I cannot tell, or perhaps I just do not want to. I crouch, pretending to search diligently for the scarf, but as soon as they are out of sight through the doorway, I stand up, my gaze travelling across the pitch. The Italians are still there, I notice, jumping, singing, their arms around each other's shoulders. With feigned indifference and a confidence I do not feel, I stroll down the staircase to lean over the railing, my elbows resting against the cold metal. I marvel at the stillness, the sense of peace that has suddenly settled over what was so recently a battlefield, the smoke seemingly only just cleared, the smell of blood and sweat still lying pungent over the stadium.

I do not know what I expect, but I am not ready to leave. Whatever else happens, I want to remember this night, to soak it in, to breathe in the sweet, intoxicating fumes of victory and elation. I want to recall how alive this game, this evening, has made me feel.

And then a shape breaks free from the group huddled together, a solitary figure with a bounce in his step jogging towards the sidelines, and however much I try to I cannot keep myself from smiling. I lean down, he reaches up, with that smirk that alights in his eyes, and I grasp the jersey in my hand. He winks at me as he jogs away, his undershirt soaked through to the tanned skin beneath, and I bury my face in the midnight-blue fabric, relishing the scent of new garment, of sweat and fight and effort, and that uncomplicated, distinctly male tinge that is so strangely familiar and simply *him*.

In the neck, just beneath the collar, there are scribbled digits in black pen. A phone number.

I find the others outside the arena, just above the staircase leading down to Wembley tube station. The crowds have ebbed out, although I can still make out a queue outside the barriers. I brandish my scarf in one hand.

"Found it!" I pronounce goofily, too exalted to allow myself to acknowledge the looks that stray to the bundled-up jersey in my other hand.

Chapter 26

I think of what to write. "Hey." *Then what?* "Great game the other night." *Like obviously, they just won the Euros.* "Thanks for the shirt, although the 10 suits you better than me." *Too cheesy?* "That was some goal. I'm so glad I was able to witness it live." *Really?*

In the end, I keep it simple.

It was great to see you again. I've missed you. And then, taking a deep breath, **Any chance you're still in town?**

My phone beeps so quickly, it is as if it has been waiting. As if the person on the other end has been waiting, too.

We're staying in London two more days before heading home, it reads. **Today will be all official meetings, Italian embassy and whatnot. Dinner Tuesday?**

Sounds perfect, I reply, almost as eagerly, my heart thumping in my chest. **What do you want to eat when you celebrate?**

I'm easy. A steak, or pasta, good wine, and good company.

The last one is already certain. Let me handle the rest, I type back, my head already brimming with ideas.

In the end, I settle on a classic: Cecconi's, in Mayfair, at a short walking distance from The Dorchester where the Italian team has their base. Dating back to the seventies when the restaurant was founded by the manager of the glamorous Hotel Cipriani in Venice, it retains that old-fashioned air of lavish luxury while the clean lines of the black-and-white striped marble floor, wide windows and white walls speaks modern chic, a concept mirrored by the menu: traditional Italian cuisine with a modern flair, always presented with an air of furtive festivity.

I am way too early, of course, my impatience getting the better of me and prompting me to forget that being 'on time' around the Mediterranean means not being more than fifteen minutes late. Pacing the street outside, my eyes firmly on the pavement, doubt gnaws at my belly. I walk around the block, trying to calm the furious, erratic beat of my heart. For a moment, I falter. What if I am being an idiot? That sensation inside, the memory of our embrace, the kiss... My mind echoes with the feeling I experienced before opening the wine bottle from Zadar, the premonition of an illusion about to shatter. What if that moment in the stadium was nothing more than the sheer euphoria of victory, adrenaline-through-the-ears elation, an instant made special only because of circumstances that will never come again?

But I the moment I round the corner and lay eyes on him, standing casually outside the restaurant, hands in his pockets and a look on his face that seems to be for no one else but me, I know it was exactly as I remembered it.

We take our time to order, so much that needs to be said taking precedence, all the blanks that need to be filled in. Despite it being a workday, the restaurant is busy, the summer now in full flow, and despite the comings and goings of the staff to refill our glasses, we are left much to ourselves. All movement revolves around the bar situated at centre stage in the dining room, smooth rounded panels of dark wood and marble, the only colour detail allowed to prevail being the unexpectedly bright green leather lining of the black chairs, calling to mind, more than anything, a Tiffany's shop window, pristine and sumptuous in what is on display, yet hinting at the clandestine in what is hidden within. I feel a sense of silly pride as Nico throws an appreciative glance around the room, nodding approvingly at the texture of the focaccia and the quality of the olive oil, at making this worthy of his success. We are celebrating as if it is the most natural thing in the world, yet initially our verbal strides towards one another are as tentative as those very first steps on the terrace in Ancona, feeling our way, finding each other again.

Armed with a bottle of Franciacorta, we crowd the table with antipasti, sharing between us a small banquet of whipped ricotta crostini, fried calamari, tartare with truffles and carpaccio topped with rocket salad and fresh flakes of parmesan.

As the waiter clears away the carnage, I lean forward across the table, my arms crossed, my belly sparkling from the wine, encouraged by the contentment of delicious food but most of all from being here, with him.

"Can I be honest?"

"Sure."

"I feel like while you know every part of my body..." A smirk spreads across his face, and I feel heat rising in my cheeks. "What?"

"Why are you blushing?" he asks, a wry smile doing wonders for his features, and I feel compelled to roll my eyes.

"I most definitely am not. Anyway, as I was saying..."

"Oh, but you are", he interjects, his elbows on the edge of the table, his chin resting on his clasped hands. "It's nothing to be ashamed of, you know. Me knowing."

"*As I was saying*", I repeat, "I'd kind of like for you to know the mind, as well..." I shoot him a grin. "But just so you know, it's quite a handful."

He studies me intently while the waiter lays the table for our main course of pasta debauchery, his eyes never leaving mine, the traces of green brought out against the dark brown.

"I've met a lot of models. Fitness bloggers, TV show hosts, actresses." It almost seems as though it is all he can do not to roll his eyes. "Every time, I just felt there was something... missing. I guess I didn't know quite what it was until I saw it in you. The drive, the ambition, the curiosity. Things I can relate to."

I cannot believe I am hearing this. *Have I just entered a parallel universe?*

"And you don't have to explain the offside rule", I joke, to hide how in absolute awe I am of his unconventional attitude, the ease with which he handles all the things about me that usually tend to frighten people away.

"Well, there is that." He smiles, and I feel the need to know something, something that has been gnawing at me since the very beginning. *Our beginning.*

"What were you doing there? Were you really visiting friends?"

"I was", he says, but I can tell by the look in his eyes there is more to it. "But the reason I was there to begin with was my grandmother. You see, she passed away last August, and I was there to settle things with her apartment."

"Oh!" I say, mortified by the thought that while he was grieving, I had been entertaining in flimsy conversation and asking for his signature, not to mention… "I'm so sorry. God, I feel terrible. Why did you speak to me at all? Why didn't you just brush me off?"

"Because it comes with the job." He shrugs. "I never turn anyone down. And you intrigued me, and then…" A wry smile plays at the corner of his mouth and a melting sensation annihilates my insides. "I enjoyed your company. And… it felt better. Visiting her home, saying goodbye, with a sense of happiness, of contentment, instead of sorrow. I had planned to go, to pay my respects if you will, but something held me back. But you… You helped me turn that day into one of hope and anticipation, rather than sadness and loss, and for that I'll always be grateful. Zadar will remain as beautiful as it has always been for me, because you made it into a happy memory."

For a moment, I am too stunned for words. *He was lonely, he was grieving, and still made time for me. Still* chose *to be with me.* The implications are staggering.

"That's quite deep for a second date", I say solemnly, smiling to take the edge off my words. I regard him thoughtfully. "Yet, in

Ancona…" I do not really know how to go on. "Why did you just leave? No note, no phone number, no nothing." He winces.

"It sounds awful when you put it like that." He rubs his neck, a gesture I now, after seeing it repeatedly over the past year, associate with him thinking, weighing his words. "Your door was closed by the time I was leaving. I knocked but there was no reply, and I didn't know whether you had already gone or if you were still asleep. I thought about writing things down, but… I can't just leave my phone number lying around. That ends up in the wrong hands and I'll never have a normal day in my life again. So I told myself it was just a one-time thing, that you wouldn't be serious about it anyway."

Which is fair, I do realise. And yet… I cannot help but wonder whether we are similar in this regard, albeit for different reasons. Whether we both have difficulty trusting. Whether it scared him, too, the overwhelming emotions we tangled ourselves in. *Did you worry it wouldn't mean as much to me as you thought it did?*

"Did you believe that?" I wonder, unable to stop myself, and he shakes his head.

"Not really. But I was afraid that since you're a fan, it might look like I was taking advantage of you."

"I'm a grown woman, you know. Not some misguided teenage fangirl. You could have asked."

Inside, my mind reels. *If that's what being taken advantage of looks like, you can do it any day.*

"I should have", he says, as if reading my mind. "I'm afraid I'm not that clever in the mornings. I realised, afterwards, that I should just have written it in your calendar." He shrugs, apologetic. "But then it was already too late."

"No", I say, reaching across the table. "It's not too late." He smiles, his fingers interlacing with mine.

With his free hand, he waves the waiter over, asking for the bill. I am about to reach for my purse but the look on his face stops me short, the borderline distasteful expression almost making me laugh.

“I did get your message”, he says, out in the cloakroom, as he drapes the coat that I do not really need over my shoulders.

“My…” I turn, not fully comprehending, but he only smiles.

“So I knew where to look for you”, he explains. “Have they revoked your citizenship yet?” I laugh.

“I think they’re still having trouble identifying me. But I daresay I can handle it when the time comes.”

“So we are going to extra time?” he asks, and I nod, biting my lip to keep from grinning too broadly.

“Extra time”, I acknowledge.

Unwilling for the evening to end, we stroll aimlessly, the July dusk pleasantly warm against our backs as we cross into Green Park and head towards the waterfront. Around us, the park has come to life, picnic blankets spread on the lawn, children chasing each other in a game of tag as the parents bring out bowls of salad, roast beef and pickles. A couple of runners, and a whole group of bikers in tight Lycra outfits, take advantage of the more forgiving evening temperature, as do an elderly couple comfortably lounging on a wooden bench, observing the passers-by. I love seeing my city like this, so open and inviting, a sense of familiarity even in this multimillion congregation of strangers. It makes me think of home, or what was once home; here and now, it is difficult to imagine any place I would rather be, anywhere that would feel more right.

“So”, I say, smiling, “tell me: are you enjoying London?” He grins at me, slinging an arm around my shoulders, holding me close.

“Very much.”

At a street corner near Victoria, we find a pub, its doors open wide to the summer, and as the sky darkens and the stars come out, we share another drink, talking, about nothing and everything, all the things that have happened between then and now, moments lost and now regained.

“I think I’ll need to get back”, Nico finally says, glancing at his watch, wincing at the sound of it, reluctance obvious in his voice. "Not that I want to."

"Me neither", I say, silently willing this night to last forever, never wanting to go home. "But I suppose I have to go to work in the morning, too." The prospect is not appealing.

"I'll go in and pay, and then we can walk back together?" he asks, and I nod, reluctantly.

"Alright", I say, hanging back as he skids up the stairs, disappearing into the throng of the pub. I lean against the handrail, tilting my head back to gaze at the sky.

"Hey there, gorgeous", a voice behind me says, and there is an unhealthy rasp to it, hoarse as if from screaming, or rusty from disuse. I turn, cautiously, to face a man, by the looks of it in his forties, unshaven, his beard unkempt and exuding a distinct odour of liquor. His eyes are small in his face, peering and unfocused. In one hand he holds a bottle, all but empty. "Fancy some company?"

"I'm waiting for someone." I sigh inwardly, ignoring him. I have seen countless drunks like him before, red-rimmed eyes and erratic movements, on the tube, on the dockside just blocks from my apartment, even sometimes, back then, outside the university, when leaving late at night.

"For me, right?" I jerk away as he grabs my arm, suddenly much closer than a moment ago. He sniggers.

"Not likely, pal", I say, hoping my voice is as confident as I will it to be. "Leave me alone."

"Ah, a feisty one, are you?" he slurs, and there is something in his eyes I do not like. "A bit of a challenge, eh?"

I try to step away once more, but his grip on my arm is too tight and there is not enough space for me to move. I look around, frantically, trying to distance myself from his foul breath as I prepare myself to kick him in the balls.

Before I have the chance, a shadow looms overhead, engulfing us.

"Hey." His voice is sharp, pitched lower than usual, and when I look up there is something fierce in his eyes. He steps in front of me, protectively, and while the supposedly independent businesswoman part of me wants to object, to say that I can deal with this myself, the rest of my soul flips over at the simplicity of the gesture, which still manages to speak volumes. At the caring, the protectiveness, the territorial instinct. "Back off."

"Hey, chill mate, I was just playing. I was just –".

"Back", he repeats, slowly, menacingly, "off." He takes a step closer, his fists clenching at his sides. "Right. The fuck. Now."

The drunk takes a step back, stumbles, not letting Nico, slowly advancing, out of his sight. He shrinks away, clearly frightened now, and finally breaks into a run. My eyes rest on Nico's back as he watches him go, the tension leaving him almost tangible as his body slowly relaxes. He wipes his hands on his trousers and turns around, finding me watching.

"Thank you", I hear myself say. "I think I could have handled him, but thank you."

He closes the gap between us, a light finger tracing my chin. His eyes are dark beneath the streetlights, unreadable. *Dear God, don't be a cliché.*

"I know you could have", he says, and I will be damned if he does not surprise me again. "That's not the point."

"What is the point, then?" I whisper as he leans over me, our noses almost touching. I am still not over how much I liked what he did, despite how much I, out of pure principle, should have resented it.

"No one touches you but me", he whispers back, and cliché or not, my hands reach around his neck, and we kiss right there, on the stairs of the pub, like nothing else in the world matters.

Chapter 27

Wednesday morning, I am in the office before anyone else; earlier, in fact, than I think I have ever been. Last night still revolving in my head, my subconscious unwilling to let go, to succumb to sleep and commit it all to memory, I am already awake at 05:00 when a text from David Lewis announces itself on my phone, asking me to see him at my earliest convenience, as we have important matters to discuss. Even in my sleep-deprived state, I understand judgement day has arrived, and I am surprised to realise I have not even thought about the entire ordeal for weeks. Now, swallowing as I open the door to his office, I feel less secure. *What if they actually have something? What if this is the end of my career, right here?* It does not seem fair, the contrast of yesterday's overpowering joy and this, the mounting sense of imminent doom.

"Take a seat", he says, not waiting for an answer as he signs off a document with a flourish and stows the heavy file away. "Good news, Sienna – I can confirm that the procedures are now officially concluded, and we can finally, with Global's blessing, proceed with business as usual." When I say nothing, he continues, "Well, good to have that over and done with", as if referring to a minor inconvenience and not a half year-long legal upheaval. "Naturally, I didn't expect anything to come out of it. All in all, I must say I think you handled it quite amiably."

Asshole, I think. The overwhelming sense of relief I should be experiencing eludes me, and I shift in my seat, a fox in a rabbit hutch, sensing a trap.

"I'm glad you came in here today, because I have a question for you." He places his hands on the desk, palms down. "Would you be willing to relocate?"

Is he trying to get rid of me? Where is this coming from? The question takes me aback. Would I be ready to move country? I do not know; I have not thought this far. *My job is here*, I tell myself. *I'll never have the same prospect of a senior position in a country where I don't speak the language.*

You mean you wouldn't move to Italy to be with your football-playing boyfriend? I hear my inner voice scoff at me. And it is right, because of course it is ridiculous. Of course I would. But I do like my independence, the sense of achievement in that I have got to where I am on my own. I am proud of what I have accomplished, and no one can take that away from me.

My boss draws me back to the present.

"Sienna, would you be willing to relocate?"

"Depends on where?" I say airily. "Milan sounds nice." He chuckles, shaking his head.

"Well, no, that's not going to be an option, as you are probably aware. The European head office is in Geneva. And I do believe you would have a nice opportunity there, one day, should you choose to."

So he's not kicking me out. What is this about?

"I'm not quite sure I understand", I say, treading carefully, bare feet on hot coals.

"Well, the fact is I would hate to let you go. This story with Sonia…" I steel myself, but he does not even miss a beat. "I just want you to know that you have my full support, as a professional, and as a person, and I wish to offer you the chance to develop that you have rightfully earned. But not in Geneva. Here."

I blink. *Did he just say what I think he did?*

"Your response to a discrimination charge is a promotion?" Disbelief taints my voice. "How on Earth will *that* look to the board?"

"Sienna, look." He leans forward, conspiratorially, his eyes glancing sideways as he drops his voice, even though there is no one here and no way anyone can hear him through the office walls. "I know there is nothing to it. I know *you*. It may have been tactless, yes, but we all have our lesser moments. I have had this promotion in mind for quite some time, but there have been internal forces acting against me. Now, I finally have leverage to do this."

I do not know how to play this game, I realise, feeling inconceivably naïve. For a moment, I think back to the after work at the pub, my old university group. Suddenly, I feel as much of a fraud now, in this room, as I did with them. I care for the science, not for the murky corporate proceedings lurking just behind the pretty veil of wealth and success.

And then, something occurs to me. Jasmine's words the day Sonia was dismissed, about how David hired her himself. About how he seldom makes blatant mistakes.

Did he use Sonia for exactly this purpose? As a pawn in a chess gambit, dispensable once she has served her cause? *Did he merely exploit a favourable situation, or did he go as far as to ask her to be obnoxious and piss me off so that he could fire her?* My head is spinning. *Did he tell her to file the complaint too, so that he had an excuse to do this? To circumvent corporate policy and push through changes they would otherwise not allow?*

It makes so much sense I feel like throwing up.

"And I would not be limited by... this, then?" I manage, stalling for time. Objectively, I can see the opportunity this entails unfolding, right before my eyes, a beautiful canvas increasingly enriched with colour, but I dare not hope it can be this simple. Yet, he shakes his head.

"You would not. This is buried now, forgotten. The position would be as Business Unit Manager, with responsibility for the entire United Kingdom and Ireland region."

I know, from the way he says it, that this is far more lucrative and prestigious than anything Dr Stevens can offer me. *Does he know more than he lets on? About the start-up, the Phase II data, the offer? Does he suspect?*

"It would be an office-based position", he continues, oblivious to my lapse in attention, "up in Finsbury, so you would be required to do less travel."

And there it is, I think. *That's the catch.* No more site visits, no more clinical trials. No more field ventures together with prominent doctors and scientists, hatching brilliant collaborative ideas over a bottle of wine. No casual stopovers in Milan for a 'check-in' at the Italian headquarters. I will be locked up in an office, my knowledge retained, all my projects transferred to someone else, all my contacts reduced to faceless emails. Making strategic decisions without any hazardous, freethinking interaction. Safe. Controlled.

The proposal of selling one's soul to the devil has never been more tangible. I clear my throat as I prepare myself.

"Thank you, David, for your generous offer." I provide him with my most dazzling smile as I stand, leaning on the back of the chair so that I, for once, am the one looking down on him. "However, I would appreciate it if you would respectfully accept my resignation in its stead, effective immediately."

With that, I walk out of his office for the last time, without so much as glancing back.

The Big Ben has just struck ten when I reach The Dorchester, relieved to find the team bus still parked outside. I tiptoe awkwardly into the lobby, feeling out of place among the grandiose neo-Roman columns and extravagant furniture, complete with golden-rimmed armchairs and thick oriental rugs. I check my watch, looking for Nico, but all I see are staff, the Italian emblem visible on their shirts as they carry heavy bags of training equipment towards the waiting transport. I walk around the foyer, scanning the huge space, ever fearful of missing anyone passing by. There is a sound from the elevator, and I jump, but there is still no sign of him. Worried he might already be on the bus, my presence going by unnoticed, I stalk back out the door, desperately scanning the dark-tinted windows, unable to distinguish any one of them from the other.

"Sienna", a familiar voice behind me says, the vowels soft and warm, yet tinged with surprise. Relief floods me as I turn, finding him there, one bag slung over his shoulder and a suitcase in his other hand, the stylised eagle of Emporio Armani in white on the blue lapel of the official team tracksuit.

"There you are", I say, trying to hide behind a light smile, but in reality, I am suddenly terrified. Of what happens once he leaves, of whether I can bear being left behind once again.

Behind him, his teammates file out of the hotel, one by one, some of them throwing us inquisitive glances, and I immediately feel horribly uncomfortable.

"I'm sorry, perhaps I shouldn't have come here." I wince, embarrassed. "I just wanted to see you before you left." *Again*, I stop myself from adding.

He sets his bag down and puts his arms around me, and I lean into him, relishing the closeness, the familiarity, the comfort. I close my eyes, breathing slowly, counting the beats of his heart.

"Don't worry", he says, finally pulling back, dropping a light kiss on my forehead. "I'm glad you came." He winks at me. "Actually, there is something I need to ask you before we go."

"What?" A soaring sensation is expanding in my stomach, but I do not know how much I dare hope.

"Will you come to Naples with me?"

"Naples?" I ask, surprised. "Why?"

"There is a special game, against Argentina. Because they won the Copa America. Europe versus America kind of thing." He shrugs, smiling slightly. "I thought you might appreciate the chance to watch us win another trophy."

"You mean you need me there to win it, right?" I shoot back, and his smile is all the answer I need.

"It will also be special for me because it's close to home. It's important to have your family near, to feel their support. In fact,

I was thinking we could go visit them afterwards. See the vineyards." He shrugs, as if it is no big deal, when it might in fact be the biggest deal of my life. "If you want."

And in that moment, I make up my mind.

"I'll come. Of course I'll come. But there's something I need to do first."

Chapter 28

I take the train up, for once not to be able to work while travelling but rather to gather my thoughts as I idly observe the passing countryside, going back in time to those days when everything was simple and straightforward. At least it seemed to be, then, before I was even aware of what the outside world beyond the seemingly evergreen hills would bring.

As the train rolls into York, the three towers of the famed Gothic cathedral rising above the tiled roofs of brown-red buildings, the familiar medieval stone walls hugging the hill, the loopholes offering fleeting glimpses of people sauntering past on their stroll around town, I search to the north for the sign in the crossroads. I think back on the dream I had, and allow myself a small smile. I do not intend to run for much longer.

The house is painted white, with the corners left their original dark wood. Rose bushes are crowding the flower beds fringed by cobblestone, thorny offshoots defying gravity to escape upwards, reaching for the rafters. An old wooden hammock sways gently on the wind, squeaking on rusty hinges, the greying canopy fabric stained beyond repair.

And the instant I lay eyes upon it, I know, with absolute certainty, that I could never have done this. While this was indeed home, once, the only home I had ever known, then, it is not anymore. It is a part of me, of my history and who I am, but it is no longer the centre of my world. Like the cosmos itself, my universe has expanded, reaching outwards, the distance between points that were once adjacent gradually increasing, their gravity progressively reduced.

I have not been back, since, and in this moment the power of distorted memories becomes abundantly clear. In my mind's eye, all of it was much grander, a quaint countryside mansion worthy of an Earl. Now, all I see is the shrunken shell of what could have been, all potential diminished, forgotten, neglect and ignorance branding what might have been homely and beautiful. Knowing what I know now, the thought of what I was willing to give up for this seems outrageous.

I ring the doorbell, anxiety coursing through me as I hear footsteps banging on the wooden staircase and the muffled shout of "Just a sec!"

Then the door flies open and there she is, oversized blouse billowing and sweatpants pulled up over her knees, light-blonde hair pulled back in a loose bun. Remnants of her baby belly are visible if not obvious, but I only focus on her face as I watch her eyes widen in horror and the door pull back away from me as she recoils.

Suddenly, I despise myself. *Is this what I've become, hostile and resentful, too frightening to even be allowed onto the porch? Is this how they see me?*

I catch the door before she can slam it shut, trying to hold her gaze.

"Please, Evelyn." I shake my head. "Please don't."

She looks at me, pupils dilated, a startled fawn ready to bolt. But at least she ceases to pull at the door, even if her hand is still on the handle, her body halfway hidden behind it, using it as a shield.

"I'm here because..." I take a deep breath. "Because it's been long enough." So much encompassed in those words, so little actually said. "And because family is important, perhaps more important than I ever realised. I wanted to offer my congratulations. And", I swallow, "if I can, my forgiveness."

She says nothing, and I can see her eyes narrowing, undoubtedly contemplating whether this is some form of trick, and I realise I need to be frank with her, if I am to have any hope of her believing me.

"I'm also here because of my mum." I venture a step closer, and she does not move away. "What you did to me, the two of you, was wrong", I say, choosing my words with care, "but how I reacted towards her was wrong too. I didn't think of it at the time, but I understand now what it must have been like for her, cut off from her closest relative, her children gone…" I trail off, trying to imagine what it would be like if Mike refused to see me. My heart aches at the mere thought; I would break in two. "Angela told her about you having a baby; that's how I knew. I would like to think that there is still something for them to repair." I steel myself; I truly never expected this day, this moment, to come. "And perhaps, there might be for us as well?"

I think back on the weekend before Christmas, when I went to Ipswich, the bitterness I felt then at the thought of reaching out. How wrong it seemed for me to be the one to do it. Watching Evelyn now, I understand it could not have been any other way. Her every movement is streaked with insecurity, a combined sense of guilt and fear that should provide me with a grim sense of satisfaction. It might even have done, once. But not anymore. All I feel now, looking at her, is pity.

"I am not here to make a fool of you, Evelyn", I say, as plainly as I can. "I am not here to hurt you in any way. I'm here to draw a line across it all, so that we both may put this behind us and continue living."

At long last, she finally loosens her grip on the doorframe, her stance still sceptical, yet considerably less hostile.

"It should be me apologising", she says, biting her lip, tendrils of her hair falling into her face. Her voice is still as I remember it, much higher pitched than mine. The voice of a young girl. "You didn't do anything… Nothing more than one would have expected, anyway. I never meant for you to discover us that way." She looks away, her nose wrinkling with shame. "I didn't think. At the time it just seemed scandalous and exciting. I never stopped to wonder what would happen when you found out."

"It's more him than you", I say, though that admittedly offers little comfort. "And I'm not sure I'll ever quite forgive that. But I am willing to forget. Or at least to move on."

"I do love him, you know", she says, a certain defiance in her voice, and I am sorry for her, sorry for the restraints she has placed on herself, the shackles with which she has bound herself to this place. I realise I know almost nothing of her adult life, what she might have wished for, once, what dreams she abandoned when she left her carefree adolescence behind.

"I'm not here to interfere with your relationship", I say. "I just think for my mother, if she knew you and I were fine… Would you speak to Angela for me? For her?"

"I can do that", she says, with a jerky nod, exhaling. "Thank you. Honestly. For coming here." She smooths her blouse down, fiddles with the hem. There are stains across her shoulder, the baby's spew likely to blame, but she does not seem to notice.

"Thank you", I say, "for listening."

We fall silent, uncertain how to proceed, the fragile truce still too new, too raw, the years to traverse still a distance too far to be accomplished in such a short space of time. She does not invite me in, and I am almost grateful: I am not sure I am quite ready.

"Say hi to Martin from me", I say, surprising even myself. "And…" I fumble for a name, having no idea how to refer to the child. "I hope to meet her, someday." Sensing we have reached the end of the line, I move to leave.

"Who is he, by the way?" she asks. I turn on the stairs, confused.

"Who?"

"The guy you've met." She raises a knowing eyebrow, but her smile is friendly. I realise I have not seen her smile in years, and how I have forgotten how much it suits her, how it lights up and renders an unprecedented charm to her otherwise ordinary face. I wonder how much reason she has had to smile in the time we have lost.

"How would you know..." At that she laughs, waving her hand.

"You have this... I don't know, *glow* about you. It sounds silly, but you seem at ease in a way." She tilts her head to one side, thoughtful. "I don't know, it's something. You seem... *yourself*. Like you never did with Martin." She winces. "Sorry, that came out wrong; I really didn't mean it like that. But it's true."

I should be mad, but I realise I am not, as if it has at length ceased to be my present and finally become my past. And maybe, just maybe, she is right. Maybe I was too naïve, and too in love, to realise he was not right for me. That he would never have seen me, accepted me for who I am, and who I wanted to be. And if I had not found them, that day, I would not be where I am today, personally, or professionally. I would never have met Nico. I find myself smiling back at her.

"You'll see", I say, winking. "Sooner or later. After all, we're family."

Sean's text drops as I roll slowly into King's Cross Station, the familiar fusion of brick castle with glass and steel hangar filling me with a calm certainty. *This is home. This is where I belong.* I think of the envelope I posted this morning, my signature on every page, the promise it entails.

I know you wanted to ask but were too polite. Well, I thought about a lot of things we spoke about, getting things done and all that, and here goes: I'm defending in September.

I smile, typing back a sign of applause. **You'll do brilliantly. If you decide you want a job afterwards, a real one, give me a call. I might be able to make you an offer not even a Welsh farm boy can refuse.**

He unceremoniously gives me the finger in his reply, but I am grinning from ear to ear and unable to stop.

Chapter 29

Also, there is a dinner party, kind of, two days before the game. You might want to bring a dress. Miss you x

"No, no, no", I say out loud as I discard garment after garment, throwing them on the bed with an increasing sense of impending doom. "Won't work. Totally won't work. Wrong. Wrong. Oh, even more wrong. Damn it."

I think of the gown his sister wore to the UEFA awards and panic inwardly. There is nothing wrong with my wardrobe, but I am growing increasingly damn certain it does not contain anything remotely like *that*. Moreover, I am even more convinced I would never be able to carry it the way Flavia did. *Fuck, why did I agree to this?*

It is mid-August and my flight leaves in two days. In desperation, I pick up the phone.

"Jasmine, hi. Hope I'm not disturbing. I was wondering whether you might be able to help me. I need a dress… And my wardrobe is a complete disaster." I bite my lip, listening. "No, it's not a date… Well, yes, I will be attending as his date, but it's not a date per se… No, it's not John. I…" I pinch the bridge of my nose, squinting. *Get a grip.* "It's a gala thing, presumably charity involved, I'm not sure. I need something not too business, not too garden party, not too Ibiza."

"Elegant, by the sound of it", Jasmine says. "And most likely designer. Come on over, and we'll get you sorted. And in return, you can explain what on Earth is going on, because this sounds like quite a story."

"I had a few in mind", she says as soon as I step over the threshold, straight out of the cab, indicating towards the hangers lined up behind her on a curtain rod. "You can choose for yourself, but my personal choice would be this one." She holds out a piece of deep azure fabric that looks frail between her hands, not to mention tiny. I run my fingers over the flimsy garment, realising from the quality it must be pure silk.

"As lovely as it looks, there's no way I'll fit into this", I say, still worried it might break in my hands. "My figure wouldn't be able to recognise an hourglass if it stood right in front of it, much less be able to emulate it."

"Oh, just you wait", Jasmine muses, directing me towards the sitting room so she can lounge on the sofa while having a full overview of my catwalk. "Save this one for last and you'll see."

I work my way through the dresses, one by one, all lovely in their own right, but not quite me. Either the colouring is too stark, better suited to Jasmine's darker, more intense complexion, or the cut is intended for more bust and less calves.

As the pile grows, I begin to despair, so when Jasmine finally hands me the blue feather-light number, I just pull it over my head without argument, in pure desperation.

Sighing, I toss my hair and turn to face the mirror – and draw to a halt.

My curves have never been much to write home about, and yet the dress falls perfectly even over my runner's body, hugging the skin in all the right places, smooth silk forming seductive shapes out of seemingly nothing. In front, the neckline is simple, yet elegant, baring shoulders and collarbones yet revealing very little else as it wraps around me with the softness of a butterfly's wing, the hem accentuated by a teasing slit that remains on the right side of provocative. At the back, though, is where the true magic happens, the V-shaped cut plunging towards my waist, and as I turn around, my hair tumbling over my almost bare back, the skirt dances around my ankles akin to heaving waves. The colour reminds me of the ocean, the mesmerising depths of the Adriatic, seen from above; enchanting, inviting, yet powerful, and treacherous. It is a masterpiece.

In silence, I spin slowly in front of the mirror, drinking it all in.

"Wow", is all I can say, and then I burst out laughing. "Fucking hell, Jasmine."

"You're a goddess", she says decidedly, her smile broadening by the second as she shakes her head. "Damn girl! That thing never looked as good on me."

"Pff, I'll believe that when I see it", I say, still spinning. I cannot get enough of it. "It's flawless. I have no idea how to thank you."

"Well, I imagine Fred might want to say hello to your man at some point", Jasmine suggests, with a wry smile. "I think that would totally make his day. He might become unbearable after that, though, but I guess I'll have to live it down. To be honest, it's a tossup between him and his father who would be most excited." I laugh.

"I'll try, I promise. We'll see what we can come up with." I give her a heartfelt embrace. "Really, you're a lifesaver. Thank you so much."

"It's my pleasure, truly." All of a sudden, there are tears in her eyes. "I still can't believe you're leaving us, that I'll come into the office next week and you won't be there. But I completely understand. After what you've been through, I wouldn't have stayed another second." She shakes her head, rubbing her eyes, and I am touched beyond imagining by her showcase of emotions. "I really don't feel like continuing to work for that creep after this, I want you to know that. But in my situation, you need the stability." I reach out, and she grasps my hand.

"Promise you'll take care. And that we'll stay in touch."

"Just you dare not to", I counter, squeezing her right back. "I'll miss you; you have no idea how much. Look after yourself, and when you decide you've had it with stability, come look for me."

"You'll do great things", she says. "I've always known that, right from the moment I met you. One day it'll be David Lewis begging you to hire him." I allow myself a malicious grin.

"Now wouldn't that be a sight? After all, they do say few things are sweeter than revenge", I say, "but I've come to realise, these past few months, the most important thing is freedom."

I think about those words for a long time afterwards, on my way home, the miracle of a dress stretched across my lap in the black London cab. There are still choices to be made, some far more difficult than those already behind me, but I cannot stop now. This is what it feels like, leaving the crossroads behind and hitting the entrance to the motorway, able to decisively push your foot down and find your own pace. The traffic all around you, the stress, the commotion, yet the sense of tranquillity that overcomes you as the indicator arrow keeps moving forwards, upwards. No longer being caught in the eye of the storm, but becoming the storm itself.

"Where are you going?"

I look up from the suitcase I am busy filling. John stands in the living room, his expression more one of confusion and disbelief than actual anger. I face him, hands on my hips.

"I'm going to Naples. Nico –", I wonder for a moment whether I ought to explain who he is, but John seems to catch on soon enough, "– has invited me to come to a game they're playing." I try to sound casual, despite the wild exhilaration in my stomach. This is all completely insane, of course, but I have made my decision, and am filled up by how right it feels.

"You're just going to run off with another guy? We're together, remember?" I sigh.

"Well, John, unless it was clear, I'm thinking that perhaps we shouldn't be."

"But it's working just fine. How can you say that?"

"John, your definition of whether it's working is based solely on whether it works for *you*. When was the last time you thought about what I wanted? Whether there was something you could do for me?"

"But you manage fine on your own. That's what you always say."

"I do, which is exactly the point. Then it becomes about how you show me you care, even when I don't need you to." I reach for another pile of folded clothes, stuffing them into the bag. "I've put you up in my apartment, despite all the inconvenience that comes with it, and you haven't even once cared to ask how I'm handling having my entire department being questioned as to whether I'm a racist bitch. How I feel about my professional reputation being publicly trailed through the mire." He recoils, as if slapped, but I am undeterred. "I think you like the idea of me more than me", I say. "It looks good on paper, doesn't it, but only as long as I fit into your life without too much effort."

As determined as I am, as disappointed as I am, the irony is not lost on me. I, who have suffered for years from a betrayal that made me unable to trust, suddenly find myself on the other side. In the role of betrayer, of harbinger of dishonesty and lies. I deliberately never told him about Nico, believing he would think less of me, believing it was in the past and did not matter. But if there is one thing I ought to know, it is that the past is always there, as a part of you, prepared to creep forward when you least expect it to, and now here we are, his disdain palpable as he sneers at me.

At least, I tell myself, *I'm being honest. I'm telling him to his face. That small thing, at least, has to count for something.*

But, it seems, counts for little.

"What more do you need?"

"Need?" I feel the frustration reeking out of me. "I need to know that it means something. That it is real. To feel, and to know that you feel something in return. We've never even had a proper row, because apparently you don't even seem to ever get angry!"

"I've always been fair to you..."

"Except when it's inconvenient for you, when I need you to be there for me and you chose not to be. But it's not even about that..."

"...and now you're just throwing it away? For what? Because of some smooth Latino thing?" He scoffs. "I never thought of you as a cliché, Sienna, so do me a favour and don't turn into one on me now."

"It's not about any 'Latino thing'". My blood is boiling, my fists clenching, my nails digging into my palms so hard it hurts. "It's about what I feel. What he makes me feel."

"You can't let your emotions control you all the time. You have to be sensible. We're living together, we –"

"We're not living together; *you* are living with *me*." I want to scream. "Because *I* helped *you* when you needed it, not because I wanted to, or because we had agreed on anything together. You can't keep expecting things from me without giving anything back."

He falls silent, and I finish packing, doing my best to ignore him even as I feel his eyes on me. The room feels deprived of air, a submarine preparing for the plunge.

"It won't last", he says, contempt dripping from his voice as I snap my bag shut. "And then you'll be replaced by some teenage chick, and the money will be gone."

"Good thing I make my own money then", I say through gritted teeth, straightening. "Seriously, do you think this is about money? Is this a joke? If you're going to insult me, at least show me the decency of doing it properly."

"Are you really willing to throw this away? There is no coming back from this, you know." I assume it is meant to sound like a threat, but the way he says it, it seems more like he is begging.

"For him, yes." I swallow, because regardless of where my feelings lie, this is not an easy thing to say. "I'm sorry, John. I really am."

"You don't even know him", he says, a hint of desperation in his voice as I pick up my bag, moving towards the doorway.

"No", I say, slowly, fixating him with my gaze until he decides to look at me. "But he knows me better than you do."

I let the door fall shut behind me, allowing myself to linger for a moment in the hallway, eyes closed as I exhale into the empty silence, but he does not open it again.

My brother drives me to the airport, any excuse to take the green Cayman out on the M25 good enough to jump on. Traffic is intense, as always, but he manoeuvres the lanes with practiced ease, barely glancing in the rear mirror as he changes gears, the subtle shift in the rumble of the engine enough, as if he is communicating with the car on a telepathic level. I have always admired the way he drives; smooth, like the stroke of a painter's brush. What Nico does with a ball, Mike does on the road, his true playing field asphalt and rubber rather than grass.

"I can't believe you're going to that game", he says, by way of conversation as he overtakes a silver Jaguar, the middle-aged balding man behind the wheel decidedly upset at this ignominy. "And that stadium! I've always thought it's one we need to visit."

"We still could, you know", I say, hating to exclude him, wishing he would come with me at the same time as I know this is on me alone. My decision, my future.

"Also, you should know I'm still recovering from all of this." He shakes his head, waving his hand about aimlessly. "I can't believe you didn't tell me."

"You'd really expect me to tell you something like that?" I ask, incredulous.

"Not all the dirty details, perhaps, but..."

"Mike!"

"Alright, alright." He holds his hand up in a gesture of surrender. "It's just crazy, you've got to admit that much." And, to be fair, I do. It is crazy, and unbelievable, and absolutely wonderful. "Speaking of nothing, have you talked to Ali recently?"

"I texted her about going to Naples and she naturally wanted a full recount later", I say, regarding him curiously. "Why?"

"I was thinking I should maybe ask her out." Mike looks apologetic, almost shy, which is so rare on him, for a moment I am at a loss for words. Then I smile, nodding.

"I'm sure she'd like that", I say. "In fact, if you want to surprise her, I know this great pop-up on Southbank you can take her to. No sensible girl would say no to oysters on the first date."

In what feels like no time, we pull up outside Gatwick Airport and Mike gets out to grab my bag from the minimalist trunk. I linger by the open door, biting my lip as I stroke the polished lacquer, the familiar rounded shape, a sudden sense of what I can only describe as wistfulness, or separation anxiety, washing over me.

"Si…" Mike hesitates, running a hand through his hair. "I know you are very capable of taking care of yourself, and I don't mean to sound like an ass, but since… You know…" He falters, both of us back in that moment, years ago, when so much changed. "I just want to make sure you know what you're doing. I don't want you to get hurt." The *again* hangs in the air between us, unspoken. He takes a deep breath. "So, are you entirely sure about this?"

"Strangely enough, I am." I do not know where this sudden confidence comes from, but I smile at him as I take my bag from his hand. He has always been good at this, I reflect – the genuine caring without overprotectiveness. Leaning forward, I wrap my arm around his neck and give him a quick kiss on the cheek. "I love you, bro." He gives me a squeeze in return, then quickly takes a step back.

"Go on, get out of here", he motions, nodding towards the departure hall. I throw him another kiss as I dash through the gates.

Chapter 30

The scene before me could have been the cover of a travel magazine, or that one advertisement that makes you buy plane tickets without thinking, just because you need to see the place with your own eyes, regardless of the cost.

Set against a backdrop of azure blue water, stone houses painted pink, peach and terracotta clutter together on the face of the cliff, seemingly clinging to each other to prevent from falling into the depths. From where I stand, on a terrace high above the rugged coastline, the winding staircases cut into the rock, leading down to secluded, pebbled beaches seem like a painting, an artist's imagination of paradise. Right outside the villa, a once-private summer residence that breathes hedonist Belle Époque luxury with its vaulted ceilings, decorative floor tiles and marble bathrooms, trees are weighed down by lemons, so close that I could easily reach out and pick one. The yellow set against the blue of the sea and sky and framed by white arcs and lush green leaves is as picturesque as it gets, the only breach in the perfect composition coming from the myriad of boats crisscrossing the ocean, beseeching the grandeur of the Amalfi Coast from below.

"Do you like it?" a voice behind me asks, and I turn, smiling. Nico is there, leisurely dressed in a pale blue shirt and navy shorts, barefoot in sleek sneakers. As he crosses the terrace, my attention is irrevocably drawn to the way the absence of his regular long socks and the cut of his pants, shorter than match kit standard, enhance the shapely outline of his sculpted legs. I bite my tongue, pretending to scrutinise the ornate wrought-iron loggias extending from the floor above to distract myself before he catches me staring.

"Like it?" I laugh in disbelief. "Nico, this is incredible. Absolutely incredible." I walk towards him, and he takes me in his arms and hugs me close. "Thank you for inviting me."

"Not at all", he says, kissing me on the cheek before directing me to a small metal table with matching ornate chairs, all painted white and facing the view. "Thank *you*, for coming."

A waiter rushes forth, spreading a white tablecloth over the gaping holes in the lace-like design of the table, and offering us a welcome cocktail on the house. Nico orders espresso and I follow suit, resulting in a nod of approval from his side. It does not take the waiter more than minutes to remerge with our coffees, as well as two frosted glasses, cold as ice to the touch, filled with bright yellow liquid.

"Limoncello", Nico explains. "A specialty in this area. It needs to be served very cold, hence we put the glasses on ice before serving. It is an old tradition, something you drink with close friends and family."

I raise my glass to his and we toast silently. To what, I am uncertain – this place? His upcoming game? Our future? The thought sends tingles down my spine. The liquor is strong and bitter, yet sweet; the cold and spirits combining beautifully to enhance the citrus tones.

"It's good", I say. "I could get used to this." He smiles.

"I guess we should talk about that, eventually", he says, looking at me intently. "Things to get used to."

Butterflies, both nervous and excited, flutter in my stomach. I have not told him about Dr Stevens' offer, about the start-up that will keep me in London for the foreseeable future, and while the last thing I want to do is ruin the moment, I know there is no way around this. I swallow, bracing myself.

"You remember I told you that I quit my job? Well, here is the thing..." I try to explain without losing myself in technicalities, holding on to the red thread of *why*. "Actually, a lot of it is thanks to you. You made me see things differently. Made me question where I was headed, what I truly wanted out of life." I smile shyly. "I'm fairly sure that wasn't your intention, but you still did. And this is something I want to do. Something I feel I *should* do."

"There are very few of us who are fortunate enough to be able to call their passion their profession", he says, nodding. "And when you feel that strongly about something, you need to follow your gut instinct. No one else can tell you what is right or wrong."

"I'm not saying work is the most important thing in my life, far from it. It's just… I've worked so hard to get to where I am, I'm not willing to give it up completely. Besides, there's…" I take a deep breath, and then I tell him. About Martin, about what he asked of me and what he promised, and what he ruined. "I just don't want anyone else to decide what I do. I need to be able to stand on my own, even when I am with someone."

For a moment, there is nothing but deafening silence, the distant waves breaking against the rocks below our feet, the soft twinkle of soothing piano music escaping from one of the windows. It is as if I can feel the cogs in my brain rotate, faster and faster, working their way around what I have just said. I feel a bit like Hugh Grant's character in *Notting Hill*, with all his friends listening in disbelief as he declares he has just turned down the girl of his dreams. *I've made the wrong decision, haven't I?*

"It's not that I wouldn't do it for you", I stumble, trying to repair, "it's just this chance might never come again and I…"

"It's okay", he says, his voice reassuring as he grabs my hand across the table, giving it a light squeeze, though I cannot read the expression in his eyes. "I understand."

What exactly does he understand? Is this it? Thoughts spiral inside me and before I feel myself freaking out, I say something completely different.

"By the way, for the Argentina game… I've noticed you always play in a much deeper position with Italy than you do with Milan.

I think you'd do better in playing higher up, to help create more, in attack. They're quite fast and great with the ball, but they're not the tallest of guys and their defence isn't exactly their strength, so you could hurt them on the counter. If you played higher up you would have a faster movement on the ball, and you could have..." I falter, suddenly not knowing how to refer to his teammates, but he seems to understand what I am getting at.

"...Lorenzo and Antonio on the wings", he fills in, his smile so bright it almost dazzles me. "You seem to really have thought this through."

"Well, it was just a reflection, I..." I shrug, self-conscious, but he shakes his head.

"No, I really like it. Perhaps you should step in as assistant coach." He winks at me.

"Assistant?" I ask with mock reproach. "You don't think I could handle being head coach?"

"I'm thinking about me", he says, still smiling. "I think it would reflect poorly on my performance. I'd be too distracted to do anything useful."

The gala dinner is held on a wide half-moon-shaped patio facing the sunset, the scatter of white sails below reflecting the soft amber glow of the fiery sky. I am reminded of Zadar, and our first sunset, the boat silhouetted as an image of pure serenity against the glaring blaze. On this level, the arches lining the open passageway connecting the heart of the hotel with the veranda represent a modern take on Hispano-Moresque architecture, rendering the villa an added air of ageless decadence. The outer walls are refurnished in a deep rust colour fringed with white, and one floor down, a cupola covered in a gold and forest green mosaic catches the rays of sunlight trickling down between the towers of surrounding buildings. Tables are set in a semi-circle, surrounding an opulent pool, the surface an aquamarine shimmer, the tabletops clad in colourful tiles, forming intricate, abstract patterns. Between them, waiters are circling, reminiscent of bees around a particularly sweet-scented flower, deftly refilling champagne glasses and offering a selection of delectable canapés served on ceramic plates painted with blue and green and yellow lemons. I drink it all in as I saunter slowly down the staircase, making a mental note to send Rachel thorough documentation of this place, knowing she would practically salivate over the colour combinations and stylistic fusion.

As soon as I step out on the terrace, it is instantly clear how perfect this dress is, the blues of the exquisite silk matching not only the maritime setting, but also the recurring theme of the décor, from the porcelain details to the curtain fringes to the tile patterns on the floor, the skirt seemingly extending as I walk, the intricate design beneath my feet creating the optical illusion of a train, spread wide like a fan.

"Sienna", Nico says by way of greeting as he steps up behind me, grinning as his eyes roam shamelessly over me. "You are truly a sight to behold." Strangely enough, I do not feel intimidated by it all – this setting, the jet set VIPs, his assessing gaze. Perhaps this dress is equipped with magical powers, emboldening me with a sense of belonging I would not normally have. I take his hand, smiling confidently.

"Come", Nico whispers in my ear. "Let me brag about you to the boys."

Milling about the terrace, I am introduced to his teammates, most of whom I have until now only seen from a distance. Leonardo Selmi, the team captain, oldest of the lot at thirty-six and inviting speculation on when his last game may be, shakes my hand with a knowing smile. He is a handsome if weathered man, one of those you can tell will age well; I can imagine him, years from now, his hair silver and his suit a dark grey, shaking hands with prominent members of the Italian football federation, or even parliament.

"You were clearly the missing piece", he says, creases forming at the corners of his eyes as he grins. "Nico has been playing well all season, but he has struggled in finals; when it truly mattered, his game wasn't quite there. Now, it all fell into place. I dare say this was his best game all season, perhaps ever."

"I'm not so sure I can take any credit for it", I say, but he shakes his head.

"You were there, weren't you? Just knowing you have a loved one in the stands, who is there for no other reason than that they care about you as a person, and not only as a player, can make all the difference in the world. The confidence it inspires can never be underestimated. It makes you attempt things you might otherwise not dare."

"And how is that?" He regards me, the expression on his face wise beyond his years.

"Because they have given you another reason to believe in yourself. The most important reason of all."

Federico Rossi, Nico's teammate from Milan and apparently an avid admirer of the local gastronomic fare, given the sheer amount of finger food crammed onto his far too tiny plate, comes over to greet me, his big hand swallowing mine as we shake. He is built the way you expect a defender to be, tall, broad of shoulder and with a bulky physique that is generally imposing, as if assembled to inspire dread in the opponent. His smile, however, is wide and friendly, his grey-blue eyes sparkling with a boyish excitement that reminds me of Mike.

"We've been looking forward to meeting you", he says, shoving his friend teasingly. "Nico has spoken of little else recently, it's become nigh unbearable." I laugh, throwing a glance at Nico who seemingly cannot decide between proud and shamefaced.

"You might be somewhat bored with the other wives, though", a tall man who Nico introduces as Filippo Vitozzi and whom I can only assume to be goalkeeper, says with a smirk. "Let's just say we don't often encounter someone with your competence and background. Not that we mind, of course", he adds, gesturing to Rossi, "as I usually have to make do with the two sole brain cells of this one."

"All of two? Filippo, I've never known you to be this generous", Nico interjects.

"We just won the Euros, after all; I'm feeling charitable", the tall man supplies, earning a loud snort from Rossi.

"Speak for yourself, Filippo", an elegant woman in a simple yet sophisticated black dress interjects, without further ado pulling me into a hug. Her bracelets and earrings dangle noisily, her movements graceful as she draws back. Her hair is black, expansive curls reminiscent of a film star from the fifties framing her lean face. "Giulia Rossi. Delighted to meet you. And don't listen too much to what these oafs are saying, some of us are perfectly able to hold a conversation with another intelligent human being." She winks. "I work for the Eataly group, manager for the northern Italy region. I hear your friend is in interior design; I'd love to speak to her sometime, see if we can bring some new ideas in. I just love the things happening on the London scene right now."

"I'm sure she'd love a project like that", I say, mentally calling out to Rachel, wishing she was here. I wish Mike was here, too, to experience all of this first-hand, to see him interact with other players on his own terms.

"Not to mention", she goes on, "we probably have other matters to discuss." She nods discreetly in the direction of Nico, jesting with Vitozzi and her husband, and raises an eyebrow. "If you ever need a crash course on what this life entails, don't hesitate to reach out."

"Thank you", I say sincerely, still not entirely certain of where to begin. "I assume you and Federico have been together long?"

"Ages", she laughs. "I was only a lowly chef then, and he came around to my restaurant every day after practice to eat my *tortellini a la panna.* He ordered the same thing every time, which is so unlike him; I assume you've already noticed how much he likes food." She rolls her eyes. "Much later, he told me it was his favourite dish, but also that he deliberately stuck to the same meal just to make sure I would notice him." She looks over at the men. "I've known Nico half a lifetime too, it seems. They have been inseparable since they were seventeen, when they met at a training camp." Her expression is full of warmth. "I don't know if I have ever seen him quite like this."

"How, do you mean?" I wonder, and she tilts her head slightly to one side, clearly pondering how to phrase it.

"Content is not the right word, because he never is. He always works the hardest, pushing himself to the limit. Fede always says he has never seen anyone so dedicated, so willing to suffer during training. But since they came back from London..." She smiles at me. "At ease", she says, eventually. "That's what it is."

Dinner, in traditional Italian fashion, Nico explains, is completely devoid of speeches, and, with its priorities in the right place, instead consists of course upon course of mouth-watering local fare: cheese, pasta, fish, meat. As trays are passed around and wine bottles uncorked, I silently marvel at the normality of these people, how unaffected by attention and fame they appear. Perhaps, I think to myself, this is not so strange after all. Perhaps this is not just a dream, a temporary fleeting fantasy, but a plausible reality.

At the very end of the evening, I manage to convince someone to take a picture of the two of us. It is a spur-of-the-moment thing, but the entire scene is so perfectly coordinated it seems staged: my dress, slightly lifted in a gust of evening breeze, shifting in all nuances of the ocean, Nico's dark navy suit harmonising with the night sky, the enchanting view spread out behind us, the fading sunshine alighting on the warmly coloured houses on the cliff. He puts his arm around my waist, his fingers gently brushing bare skin, and for an instant I turn slightly towards him, a wide, genuine smile on my face as our eyes meet and the camera flashes. It is one of those photos that not only says more than a thousand words but manages to stop time, to encompass true emotion.

I send it to Jasmine, screaming out my thanks in writing. **The dress! PERFECTION. x**

POWER COUPLE! comes her reply, and all questions still to be answered, all loose ends aside, I allow myself to think that maybe, just maybe, we might be.

Chapter 31

The stadium is a sight to behold, the blue theme of the stands, representing the Napoli club colours, repeated in the running track circumventing the pitch itself. It is sold out, as far as I can tell, a wide-open colosseum scintillating in shades of blue, from the cerulean of the Italian ocean to the pale Argentinian sky. The setting is symbolic for both these nations, given Diego Maradona's status as both local club legend and national hero, and I notice a fair number of shirts bearing his name among fans on both sides. Flags are hung from the balconies of the buildings visible beyond the stands, apartment value on the upper floors markedly increased on match day, and from the speakers, Edoardo Bennato and Gianna Nannini's decades' old World Cup anthem is blasted across the arena, promising to enfold us in a magical Italian summer night. The air is hot, humid, the sky on fire in orange gold. The game is intense, yet come halftime no team has managed to break the deadlock.

Approaching the fifty-minute mark, the Italian head coach checks his watch, signalling to the fourth official who brings out the sign announcing changes to be made. A whisper seeps through the crowd as the screen shows number six, for the team's irrefutable leader.

And as the man I have previously only thought of by last name, but has now, through Nico's eyes, come to see only as Leonardo, is summoned to change, he waves Nico over. I watch, entranced, as he pulls the captain's armband from his arm and onto Nico's, giving him a slap on the back as he walks off the pitch. Applause erupts as he acknowledges the crowd, waving his arms in salute. Behind him, Nico adjusts the armband over the sleeve of his shirt, the stark white gleaming against the azure blue.

"It's the first time he's worn it, right?" I lean over and ask the man next to me, trying to sound casual, like any other spectator. It is, to the best of my knowledge, but I still want to hear him say it.

"It is", he nods, "and well in time too. Can't imagine Selmi will stay on in the national team that much longer, especially not now, after the Euros. He must be fairly content with his career. But Di Luca taking over is a good choice. He has that something, you know."

"Yeah", I agree, forcing the nervous laughter down my throat at all the *somethings* this man could never imagine. "He certainly does."

As if on cue, my eyes stray to Nico, and it is as if he is trying his hardest to prove the man right. There is a new authority in his gestures, a different sense of purpose in his movements. The team revolves fluently around him, following his direction, in a way I have not fully experienced before, and something growls in my stomach. A sense of pride at how natural his leadership is, how readily they listen to him, but there is also something else. Something feral, that I do not recognise myself, that heats my blood from within.

"Look at him", my neighbour beckons, startling me out of my reverie. "It's like he was made for this role. Like he's been waiting for the chance."

And then I see how he takes Conterno and Costa – *Lorenzo and Antonio* – to the side, gesturing. Their nods, followed by deliberate progression up the pitch, advancing their positions. My heart swells with pride, almost boiling over. *Perhaps you should step in as assistant coach.*

Minute by minute, Italy take over, their higher press throwing Argentina, rushing their decisions, forcing them into making mistakes. Time and again, the home team steals the ball, and when Nico finally receives it in the final third, he launches into attack by himself.

It is a spectacular run, all the way into the penalty area, where the Argentinian defence is crowding the space like hyperactive ants. Nico feints, feints again, trying to find an opening, performs an overstep but the defender goes the right way, and then…

A collective gasp seeps through the crowd as his right leg swings behind his left and his right foot connects with the ball, sending it in a beautiful wide arc above the heads of the Argentines and into open air, where there is nothing but the forehead of Rossi – *no*, I correct myself, *Federico. Fede.* – and the empty hands of the goalkeeper as the ball rattles into the net.

The stadium erupts.

Mount Vesuvius could have staged a comeback worthy of a second Pompeii in this very moment, and it would most likely have gone unnoticed. The roar of the crowd is deafening, someone far too close is blowing a horn that annihilates my eardrums, flags and scarves are sent flying and from the outside comes the honking of car horns. It is absolute madness, and I am in the middle of it all, screaming myself hoarse even as my hearing ceases to function.

"*Mamma mia*!" the man next to me is shouting, equal parts in ecstasy and to be heard over the rumble. "What a performance!" Two rows down, Giulia Rossi turns towards me, her expression priceless, an open-mouthed, awestruck *Wow.*

"A *rabona*", I say, feeling pride and awe seeping through my body. "A *rabona* assist. I can't believe he did that."

"Ah, so that's what it's called, that move." The man nods. "I thought that was a dance step, though? In tango?" He suddenly looks somewhat apprehensive. "We used to dance, my wife and I, when we were younger; that's how I thought of it."

"No, it is", I agree. "They actually named the dance step after this." I wave towards the pitch, suddenly remembering Mike and I, more than fifteen years ago, in the scruffy neighbourhood backyard after dark, under the pale industrial lights, practising ridiculous Ronaldinho skills that no mere mortal could get away with doing in an actual game. Or so we thought. At the same time, Leonardo's words from the other night come back to me, about daring, and inspiring confidence.

This was his dream move, I remember, recalling the interview I listened to, what seems like half a lifetime ago. *A* rabona *in an important game.* All kinds of sensations are simmering in my stomach, but most of all, there is this ridiculous, giddy happiness that I have not felt in a long time.

I stand as soon as I hear the door to the hotel room slam, a grin spreading all over my face as he walks in, still in match gear, captain's armband and all, not even showered, and swoops me up in a long, firm embrace.

"Congratulations", I whisper, inhaling the smell of hard-earned sweat, but also that distinct scent of him that somehow seeps through it all. My hands clasp around his neck. "You were incredible." Then I pull back, a mock frown on my face. "Though clearly in all your amazingness you didn't bother to clean up?"

"I came straight here from the stadium", he says, with a pointed look. "I made Leo do the press conference. I just couldn't wait to see you. It was the only thing on my mind, to share this with you. Since you came with me."

I would object, if it did not feel so ridiculously good to hear him say this.

He starts to pull the armband off his arm, but something in me stops him.

"Wait", I hear myself say, as if from somewhere distant, where I can safely observe this sudden boldness that has come over me. I bite my tongue as I cock my eyebrows at him. "Leave it on."

A dangerous gleam alights in his eyes as he pulls me closer.

"Oh, so you like this, do you?" he murmurs, weaving his hand through the hair behind my ear and letting his lithe fingers trail down my neck, and I smirk.

"Actually, I do", I say, resting my hand on his forearm, tracing the veins that show beneath the skin, the tight piece of elastic snug around his muscles, reminiscing the pride I felt when I saw him pull it on, the sudden fierce hunger in the pit of my stomach. "*Captain.*"

He smiles then, a wicked, glorious smile, and I know in that moment that there is no turning back. There is nothing else but this, the tightening of the air, the raw physical awareness of another's presence, the immediate and irrevocable knowledge that he need only ask, and I would do it, do anything, and not only do but beg him to let me.

His touch is light as a feather on my skin and the echo of my heartbeat resonates like that of a drum, the mounting rhythm matching the rising elation in my chest as his hands unravel what remains between us. My fingers slide up his neck and into his hair, tangling in those soft curls, and as I bring my mouth to his, his slender hands rest on my hips, pulling me close enough to feel, feel everything, every part of how our bodies fit together. His lips move to my neck and in the air that is suddenly allowed to rush into my lungs, I release a sigh that comes out as a soft moan against his throat.

Without warning he hooks his leg around mine and I feel the bedsheets against my back as we topple over.

"Your second *rabona* of the night, was it?" I grin at him, and there is laughter in his eyes.

"Oh, you noticed that one, did you?" he whispers in my ear, his words echoing inside my skull, a low, pleasant reverberation. "Except this one was even better than the first."

"Because that was just an assist, and now you get to score?" I tease. "So cheesy."

"I'm Italian", he shrugs. "It is expected of me." His hand slides down my waist, his forehead resting against mine, so that I can see every fleck of green in his eyes, every trace of emotion, so close I think I might disappear within their depths and never resurface.

There is so much heat in this moment it seems impossible that the room does not catch fire, yet I feel myself shaking, the trembling sensation of being undone from within. It is as if there is not enough blood in my veins, nor is it moving fast enough, to be at all the places it needs to be to give way to all the sensations yearning to simultaneously spring forward. I almost want to laugh, and even as I choke the absurd notion down, I feel him smile against my skin, feel his lips skid across my stomach, as if he knows exactly what he does to me and will make it last for as long as he can, out of pure satisfaction, or plain spite – I cannot tell and I am no longer sure there is a difference.

And despite the proximity I still cannot resist bringing him even closer, my hand nestling in his hair, its velvety ringlets as smooth and gentle as his tongue, the release of a wave crashing over our heads tangible in the strength of the grip with which I hold on to him. And even as my breathing slows and he looks up at me through the haze with that confident, mischievous smile, I feel my entire body ache for him, and realise that this, finally, *this* is what it truly means to want someone.

Chapter 32

There is a sound from his phone, and he groans, rolling over. The beams of sunlight falling in through the window drapes over him as he does, rendering his skin golden as he hunches forward, frowning as he reads. Somewhere outside, there is the call of a seagull, the distant rolling of waves against the cliffs. The curtains flail against the open slit between glass and frame, traces of citrus and wild herbs on the air. I stretch, my palms pressing against the cool marble headrest. My body should be tired, worn-out, yet I have rarely felt more alive.

He drops the phone and falls back on his stomach, leaning on his elbows. His hair falls into his eyes, and he smiles. *That smile. That damn smile.* He is, right here and now, without a shadow of a doubt, the most beautiful thing I have ever seen.

"What was it?" I murmur as I let my hand roam shamelessly through his hair and down his neck.

"Nothing that can't wait", he says, yawning. "Just my agent being overeager, as usual."

"Oh?" I say. "What about?"

"There has been some interest from other clubs." He shrugs. "I don't know, maybe it's time for a change."

"What clubs?" I ask, leaning on my elbow. He traces circles on the sheet with elegant fingers.

"Several", he says, "but I'm considering Chelsea." His voice reveals nothing, but when his eyes meet mine there is something there that I cannot put into words. I only know that it fills my insides with an undeniable warmth.

“I’m thinking we could see each other more often, that way”, he says, still as casual. “If you want.”

“You would do that for me?” I croak, because that warm feeling inside is suddenly crowding my throat and I find I cannot swallow properly.

“Sure”, he says, taking my hand and lightly kissing my fingers. “But first, we will have vacation. And this will always be home.”

He asks the valet to bring about the car for the drive down to the vineyards, and I wait while he dashes off, closing my eyes against the brightness of the sun, the heat of its rays a balm against my face, an expectant feeling settling in my chest. My phone buzzes, Rachel’s text reading **Update?! Is it obscenely amazing or do you need me to come get you?** I send her the pictures, launching into a recount that is as revealing as I can possibly manage in as many words.

There’s so much more I need to tell you, I add, mentally blowing her a kiss.

As soon as you’re back, you’re mine, she writes. **For now, though, enjoy yourself.** I smile, the echo of our conversation almost a year ago in the back of my mind. Only this time, I believe her.

There is a low growling rumble, and I turn around just as the tyres screech against the asphalt when brought to a halt right in front of us. The valet steps out, handing over the keys to Nico with the faintest of polite bows.

I roll my eyes, even as a smile spreads over my face and I cannot hold it back.

“What?” he says, and for a moment I am reminded of our first night, that trace of hesitation, that passing sense of insecurity.

“Of course”, I say, smiling wider. “*Of course* it’s a Ferrari.”

He laughs, then, motioning a bow. I run my fingers along the perfectly smooth lines, the bright red lacquer.

“You know they used the same aerodynamic simulation programs for this as for the Formula 1 cars?” I say, still examining the curves, the minute attention to detail in the design. "You see Pininfarina's style so clearly in this. Sharp, yet flawless. The Enzo and the Roma, and back then, the F50, are all a bit extreme, all harsh pointed angles and rough lines, but I love the curves of the Modena. This is a great choice. Elegant." I glance up, wink at him. "Smooth, like that free kick of yours."

He raises an eyebrow in surprise. Without a word, he opens the door on the driver's side, and I feel my heart drop through my stomach and down to my knees.

"You want me to drive?"

"I would consider it an honour, given your expertise." He is smiling, relaxed, leaning against the car, his white shirt unbuttoned at the neck, the breeze clutching at his hair. I drink in the view, still in disbelief that this is happening, that this is real.

"Why, if you insist", I shoot back, even as my heart races from zero to a hundred in half a second. My hands slide over the exquisite leather of the seat, the Formula 1-shape steering wheel, the steel transmission, the Testarossa-inspired side mirrors. Then the engine growls to life beneath us, a wild animal willing to be set free, and we are off, along the winding roads, the cliffs rising above, the turquoise ocean far below. The wind pulls at my hair, the smell of salt and sea and the heat of the asphalt rising to a quivering haze as we rush past, as if we are driving into another dimension. I push down on the accelerator, the purr of the engine like that of a satisfied cat, urging me to let it go, so that it may show me what it can do.

I can feel him looking at me, and I glance over as his fingers lace together with mine over the stick shift, its sheen like silver in the sunlight, but his words are lost in the roar of the engine.

~